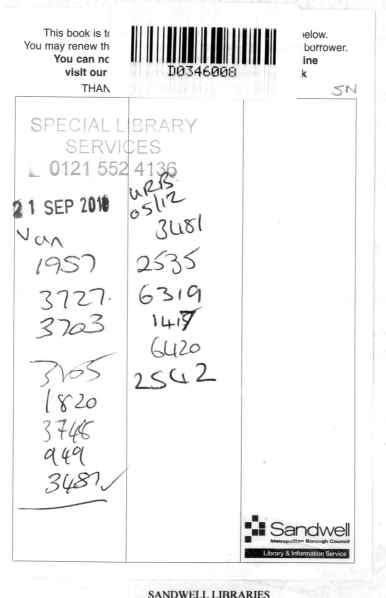

This book is to ...below.
You may renew th... borrower.
You can no... **ine**
visit our ... **k**
THAN...

SN

URBS
05/12

Van
1957
3727.
3703

3765
1820
3745
949
3487 ✓

3481
2535
6319
1417
6420
2542

EIGHT WEIRD TALES

A curious woman investigates the dark secrets harboured within the ancient chapel of a ruined signal station. An antique ivory hunting horn will spell the downfall of Professor Goodspeed. Meanwhile, an eldritch voice draws a lonely man ever closer to the drowned town of Lod ... Eight short tales, each directly inspired by a master of the mysterious or supernatural — Arthur Conan Doyle, H.P. Lovecraft, Anthony Hope, or M.R. James — which will send chills down your spine ...

Books by Rafe McGregor
in the Linford Mystery Library:

THE SECRET SERVICE
THE SECRET POLICEMAN
THE SECRET AGENT

RAFE MCGREGOR

EIGHT WEIRD TALES

Complete and Unabridged

LINFORD
Leicester

First published in Great Britain

First Linford Edition
published 2010

British Library CIP Data

McGregor, Rafe.
  Eight weird tales. - -
(Linford mystery library)
1. Supernatural- -Fiction.
2. Large type books.
I. Title II. Series
823.9'2–dc22

ISBN 978–1–44480–382–2

Published by
F. A. Thorpe (Publishing)
Anstey, Leicestershire

Set by Words & Graphics Ltd.
Anstey, Leicestershire
Printed and bound in Great Britain by
T. J. International Ltd., Padstow, Cornwall

This book is printed on acid-free paper

To:
Lisa Claire Buckle
and
Rachel Louise Dawson

Contents

Introduction

The common thread running through the eight tales in this volume is that they are all directly inspired by the work of a great master of mystery and supernatural fiction. In some of the stories the derivation is obvious, in others more obscure, and I shall leave it to each reader to decide which of these four authors provided the material I used as my source.

Sir Arthur Ignatius Conan Doyle (1859–1930): Despite being a prolific writer of fiction in several genres, Conan Doyle is best known as the creator of Sherlock Holmes. Holmes has been portrayed by seventy-five actors in two hundred and eleven films to date, more than any other character real or imagined. A 1995 survey estimated twenty-five thousand books, films, plays, and games featuring Holmes, published and performed in thirty-five different languages.

Montague Rhodes James (1862–1936):

M.R. James was the Provost of King's College, Cambridge (and later, Eton), a respected medieval scholar, and an authority on Bible apocrypha. He wrote comparatively little fiction, but his forty-odd ghost stories are acknowledged by numerous experts as being the most influential in the English language. They are also pretty scary.

Sir Anthony Hope Hawkins (1863–1933): Anthony Hope's first swashbuckler, *The Prisoner of Zenda*, was an instant success in 1894. Although the novel inspired a host of imitations, and even creating a literary subgenre (the Ruritanian Romance), the series was doomed by the tragic end of the sequel, *Rupert of Hentzau*, which dissuaded David O. Selznick from capitalising on the success of his 1937 blockbuster of *Zenda*. Instead, he started work on a film called *Gone with the Wind*. Had he filmed the sequel to *Zenda* ... the possibilities are limitless.

Howard Phillips Lovecraft (1890–1937): H.P. Lovecraft scraped a living from selling short stories to *Weird Tales* magazine and ghostwriting for the less talented. In spite of the fact that he never had a novel or anthology published in his lifetime, Stephen King is one of several successful speculative fiction authors that regard Lovecraft as the most influential horror writer of the twentieth century.

Sadly, it has been more than seventy years since the last of these great story-tellers died, but their legacy lives on in countless reprints and imitations of their work. Imitation is, after all, the highest form of flattery, and it is with the utmost respect that I offer these eight stories as a homage to my betters.

Rafe McGregor
York, 2008

The Letters of Reverend Dyer

Whitby, Oct.31. 1821
The Rev. W. Buckland D.D., F.R.S.
Dear Sir,

I beg you will forgive this unsolicited correspondence. I write to you not only as the foremost authority on geology in Great Britain, but also as a man of God, a vocation which I am very proud to share. I read with great interest 'The Connexion of Geology With Religion Explained', and found your conclusion that the new science provides irresistible proofs of an Universal Deluge both erudite and reassuring. It is my conviction that close investigations of the works of Omnipotence are part of the homage due to the Creator, and that as His works are explored by the light of science, so His infinite perfections are more and more revealed.

I would like to inform you of what I believe is the most entire specimen of a saurian animal thus far discovered. I am sure you are well aware that the coast near Whitby is abounding in petrifactions and not a few antiquities, and it is the habit of my colleague, Mr. Marshall White, and I to prospect the cliffs for fossilised remains. A fortnight ago, in the midst of an uncommonly bracing sea breeze, we unearthed the skeleton in the compact shale of the scar between Whitby and Saltwick. The fossil exhibits, on a Cyclopean scale, the remains of the specimen found in the same location by Captain Chapman, as well as certain other, unique, features.

The entire petrifaction measures exactly forty six feet if extended at length; but only occupies forty feet, six feet of the tail being bent back. It shows one hundred and forty four vertebrae, each approximately seven and a half inches across. The skeleton includes part of both pectoral fins, and part of one of the smaller fins. The former are of great interest for they stretch to an astonishing thirty feet. Their situation is also higher up the barrel-shaped girdle than usual, and would suggest wings with serrated edges were it not obvious that this is a marine creature. The latter fact is confirmed by the extraordinary skull. The head is nine feet long and has five appendages suggestive of a cephalopod, with flexible arms or tentacles extending almost six feet beyond the jaws. The shape of the cranium also differs from previous specimens, as my crude illustration attempts to show.

I take comfort in the animal as confirmation of the exquisite orderliness and diversity of Divine creation, and find my faith in the perfect purpose of our Father in Heaven revitalised. I hope our discovery will be of interest, and beseech you to accept this as an open invitation to view the fossil form should you return to Yorkshire.

I wish you every blessing in our Lord Almighty.

Yours respectfully,
Winfield Dyer

★　★　★

Whitby, Nov. 13. 1821
The Rev. W. Buckland D.D., F.R.S.
Dear Sir,

Please accept my sincerest thanks for your kind reply, which I received on Nov. 10. I present a summary of my attempts to ascertain precisely what type of saurian Mr. White and I found. Mr. White has been indisposed since my last letter, suffering from a severe cold he caught during our excavation of the skeleton. The wind was particularly pitiless, howling as it hindered our every step, and I consider myself lucky not to have been similarly afflicted. Having contemplated the creature for some time, I feel a curious certainty that the fossil has exceptionally antiquated origins, and have decided to name it PALAEOSAURUS.

The idea of the sea crocodile or alligator described by Captain Chapman has of course been discredited in favour of the lizard, now styled ICTHYOSAURUS by Sir Everard Home, Bart. With this in mind, I examined the imperfect drawings and descriptions of Captain

Chapman's discovery in 1758, as well as those of ICTHYOSAURUS fossils found in the last thirty years. The largest of these, the dimensions of which we may only deduce from the size of the vertebrae, is approximately thirty feet in length. The PALAEOSAURUS is too dissimilar in size and shape to share a common genus.

I next turned to MOSASAURUS, the Beast of Maastricht unearthed in 1780. The five feet long jaws of the fossilised skull found by Canon Godin are close in size to the PALAEOSAURUS, although there is no evidence of any appendages attached to the maw of the former. I corresponded with Mr. Adriaan Camper, the naturalist who first proposed the beast was a lizard, and await his reply. I also solicited the assistance of the Rev. William Conybeare to enquire whether the creature could be of the same species as his lately discovered PLESIOSAURUS. I believe this is a marine reptile with a large jaw that propelled itself by the use of flippers resembling wings. Until I receive more information from either of the aforementioned scholars, I am inclined to agree with the hypothesis of Mr. Camper's father, who proposed that the MOSASAURUS was a species of whale.

I have been sorely troubled by my lack of success in classifying the saurian, and have suffered a commensurate loss of sleep. What rest I have had has been haunted by dreams of sea dragons in the abysmal slime, and I look forward to Mr. White's return to health, for his assistance has been invaluable.

I wish you every blessing in our Lord Almighty.

Yours respectfully,
Winfield Dyer

★ ★ ★

Whitby, Nov.24. 1821
The Rev. W. Buckland D.D., F.R.S.
Dear Sir,

Rev. Conybeare was commendably prompt in his response, and has expressed his desire to travel to the North Riding to see the PALAEOSAURUS as soon as he is able. He was also quite clear that the dimensions of the animal preclude it being a PLESIOSAURUS, which grows to one third of the size at most.

The PALAEOSAURUS fossil has caused me to question the age of the globe once again. The examination of the character of the crust of the Earth has thus far proved beyond all doubt the existence of the Deluge suffered by Noah. The geological facts, especially the discovery of such a large number of marine creatures embedded in the depths of the stratigraphic rock, confirm the sacred Scriptures. My own calculations closely match those of Professor Ussher, of Trinity College, Dublin, who dated the beginning of the world to 4004 BC, and proved that it was created by our Lord in six days, as described in the Book of Genesis.

I find the theories of men such as the Comte de Buffon unpalatable. His assertion that the Earth is some sixty eight thousand years older, and that it was created in seven epochs as opposed to seven days is ludicrous, unsupported by independent scientific evidence, and unworthy of a natural philosopher. Although I know that unverified attempts to extend the period of creation to such lengths are irresponsible, and detract from the honours of the Almighty, I find myself assailed by doubt.

Mr. White and I have reassembled the PALAEOSAURUS in a modest repository on the quayside in order to conduct a more thorough investigation of its properties. Mr. White's health is fully restored, but he has informed me that he will have nothing more to do with the saurian. When I asked why, he mentioned nightmares, and I did not press him further. As a result of this temporary hiatus in our professional collaboration I have spent many lonely hours examining the skeleton. I cannot but acknowledge the eldritch aura of a great and venerable age that predates the ICTHYOSAURUS by centuries, even aeons, as if the PALAEO-SAURUS is some sort of elder thing.

Perhaps Mr. James Hutton was correct and six thousand years is not enough time for the formation of the Earth, and for creatures such as this to die out. But, if

Mr. Hutton or the Comte de Buffon are right, what does this mean for religion, and our belief in the Heavenly Father? Such questions vex me for the first time in my life, and I have spent the last few evenings walking along the shore at Saltwick, in the hope of finding the answers I seek. So far, all my efforts have produced is a case of the sniffles, which has caused a trilling in my ears reminiscent of the ululation I first heard on the wind more than a month ago. I eagerly await Mr. Camper's reply.

I wish you every blessing in the Lord Almighty.

Yours respectfully,
Winfield Dyer

⋆　⋆　⋆

Whitby, Nov. 27. 1821
The Rev. W. Buckland D.D., F.R.S.
Dear Sir,

Please forgive my impertinence in writing again so soon, but I feel an urgent need to confide the fears that the PALAEO-SAURUS has provoked in my heart and soul, indeed in my very faith in the King of kings. As a priest and a scientist, you are my only avenue for confession. I beg you will give me a patient hearing, and that you will not condemn my remarks until you have candidly weighed them, for I cannot admit to anyone else that the longer I look upon the PALAEOSAURUS, the more I doubt the benevolence of the Divine.

We must accept that scholars have not obtained sufficient data for satisfactorily explaining the natural causes, employed by the Creator, to bring the globe to its present state, which, as all agree, is widely different from its original state. Nonetheless, I cannot conceive of how an omnipotent and altruistic God could allow one of His creations to fail. If we, men and beasts alike, are all His creations, how could our Father approve the extinction of a creature begotten by His own Grace? I feel this is decidedly true of an awe-inspiring monster like the PALAEOSAURUS. Surely Providence should preserve such a powerful, admirable thing?

I know there are only two possibilities:

1. The Lord God is as we believe, and the PALAEOSAURUS is not extinct, but lives in some deep and mysterious part of the sea, far away from the eyes of man.
2. The PALAEOSAURUS and the other sea dragons are extinct, and the Lord is not as we are told in the Bible, but created the Earth as some jest or mistake.

As a rational man, I repudiate the latter conclusion, and accept that the oceans are populated with a great variety of saurians. It will be argued, as a formidable objection against my theory, why, if these sea creatures are not extinct, are there no remains of quadrupeds or men found with them? If, in most instances, what was dry land before the Deluge became the base of the sea after it, and vice-versa, this is sufficient reason for the organic remains of our present strata to consist chiefly of marine productions. The remains of land animals would be chiefly imbedded in the strata which now compose the bottom of the ocean, and men, in the face of the gradual rising of the sea, would have used their superior intellect to retreat to the higher ground.

I expressed my belief that the old ones live in the oceans to Mr. White, without divulging my crisis of faith. He replied that there are certain things which are better left undisclosed, and times when ignorance is in fact preferable to knowledge. Thereafter he immediately excused himself, and I have not had the opportunity to question him on what is a most peculiar sentiment for a man with such an enquiring mind. While Mr. White has recovered from his ailment entirely, I appear to be suffering from influenza. I heard a particularly clear ululation while I was walking on the West Cliff yesterday and I had a fancy it was an Elder Thing calling to me.

I wish you every blessing in the Lord.

Yours respectfully,
Winfield Dyer

★　★　★

Gate Helmsley, Nov.30. 1821
The Rev. W. Buckland D.D., F.R.S.
Dear Sir,

Now that Mr. White has betrayed me, there is no one else to whom I can turn.

I present a summary of my attempts to ascertain precisely what the ramifications of the discovery of the PALAEOSAURUS are.

1. <u>Facts and Inferences</u>:

A. There is strong general ground for presuming that the globe was so long immersed to effect the most important changes in its crust.

B. Thus, as the ocean subsided after the Flood, new strata rose, experiencing in their rise those breaks, ululations, and other irregularities, with which they are marked.

C. The PALAEOSAURUS is an Old One, a race that lives in the deepest sea and created the Ubbo-Sathla, the primordial inhabitants of the Earth.

2. <u>Hints and Conjectures</u>

A. The greatest antiquity is God Himself, for God alone predates the creation of His Earth.

B. God alone is immortal, but is not necessarily alone.

C. The PALAEOSAURUS is immortal, but for the specimen at Saltwick, which was murdered by a Shoggoth.

3. <u>Conclusion</u>
The PALAEOSAURUS is one of a race of gods!!! <u>A dead god</u>. The Old Ones are neither benevolent nor malevolent, but unconcerned with humanity, their true motivation as fathomless as their submarine cities.

I am sure you will agree with me when I pronounce that reality as we know it is a beguiling veneer, and that the truth must be exposed by all means.

I wish you best of luck in the Old Ones.

Yours respectfully,
Winfield Dyer

★ ★ ★

Whitby, Dec. 1. 1821
The Rev. W. Buckland D.D., F.R.S.
Dear Sir,

I beg you will forgive this unsolicited correspondence. I write to you not only as the foremost authority on geology in Great Britain, but also as a man of God, a vocation which I am very proud to share. It is my unpleasant duty to report that Rev. Dyer was confined to a lunatic asylum near York three days ago. I believe he has communicated with you since. I have instructed the superintendent to prevent any further such attempts, and ask that you will ignore any letters received. I arrived in Whitby five days ago to find the Rev. raving and ranting in shocking and blasphemous terms, his mind cracked, and in no state to look after himself. I assisted Mr. Marshall White, who was concerned for the Rev.'s welfare, in arranging for his certification and committal.

I then returned to the original purpose of my sojourn, the study of the cyclopean creature called PALAEOSAURUS. It is an awe-inspiring specimen, by the far the largest and most complete of any saurian I have seen. There is also the sense of great antiquity to which Rev. Dyer quite correctly referred prior to his incipient mania. My attempts at classification were hindered by a lack of rest last night, caused by a merciless wailing in the wind.

I have repaired to lodgings set well away from the seafront and I anticipate resuming my investigation of the PALAEOSAURUS tomorrow. I am impatient to expose its secrets.

Yours respectfully,
William Conybeare

The Adventure of the Long Man

A Reminiscence of Roderick Langham.
Late of the Indian Army and the
Metropolitan Police Force

It took me thirty-six hours to track the Macedonian to a village inn, in Sussex.

My arrival late on a Friday night and my haggard countenance both lent plausibility to my masquerade as a City stockbroker seeking a tranquil weekend in the country. I was just in time to join the other guests for supper, and our landlord — a *Signore* Rossi — introduced me to all four of my fellow-lodgers, including Makedonski. I was seated next to Edford, a cadaverous professor of European History at Brasenose College, Oxford. Without prompting, he confided that his true passion was archaeology, the practice of which had brought him and his two students to the South Downs. Hughes was a Welshman who didn't look old enough to be at university, small, dark and surly. Parker was tall, fair, and full of his own self-importance. Either Edford was gregarious by nature, or perhaps tired of the company of younger men, for he spoke without respite.

Only he and I repaired to the parlour for brandy and cigars, the others retiring upstairs. Rossi set a decanter of armagnac on the side table, and asked if there were anything else we required, or if we wanted the fire lit.

We both replied in the negative, but I asked, 'Do you have any cats about the premises.'

'*No, no, Signore.* Not in the inn.'

'Thank you, a very good night to you.'

'*Buonanotte.*'

'What's the matter, Langham, do they give you hay fever?' asked Edford.

'No, I can't abide the creatures. Vermin.'

As our host retreated, Edford leaned closer to me and said in a conspiratorial tone, 'Did you know he's quite the red, our *Signore* Rossi?'

I was nonplussed, but didn't want to show it, so I merely said, 'Oh?'

'Absolutely. He was one of Garibaldi's Redshirts in the Austro-Sardinian War.'

'Really?'

'Yes. Rather curious, don't you think?'

I did, but feigned innocence. 'Is it?'

'Well, there he was fighting for a new Italy all those years ago, and now he's living abroad. It doesn't seem right for a nationalist to be an expatriate. It wouldn't surprise me if the fellow was an exile, on the run . . . '

It didn't take me long to realise that Edford was not only garrulous, but inquisitive to the extent of being rude. Naturally I was used to such interrogations, albeit with a far more sinister motive. I kept to the truth wherever possible and subtly turned the focus of the conversation back to his hobby of archaeology. I knew very little about the discipline — if indeed it could be called such — and was quite content in my ignorance, but Edford's impromptu lecture served a dual purpose: it facilitated my continued observation of the inn's entrance, and kept him from asking questions I didn't want to answer.

By a quarter past eleven, there was still no sign of Makedonski. I was considering turning in, but I knew I was too tired to sleep, and hadn't drunk nearly enough brandy to subdue my feverishness.

'I say, you don't fancy a walk up to the Wilmington Giant, do you? I suffer terribly from insomnia, so I always take some light exercise before going to bed. I stroll over every night to check on our dig and smoke a last pipe.'

'The Wilmington Giant?' I asked.

'Yes, the chalk figure carved into Windover Hill. I'm excavating at its feet, so to speak. It's only a mile away.'

I assented and we set out into a cool, crisp, June night, under a glimmering moon. I'd hoped the fresh air would sooth my frayed nerves, but its effect was quite the reverse. We took a winding course from the inn to Wilmington Street, and the undulating landscape was filled with shadows alien and ominous in shape. Edford waxed lyrical on the respective abilities of his two students, and his

high-pitched voice exacerbated my agita-
tion. I tried unsuccessfully to block out
the sound.

' . . . I didn't mention that Parker is the
eldest son of Sir Roger Bart, of Melford
Hall, did I? I try and avoid it, you see,
because the fellow's rather too big for his
boots as it is. He's a passable Classics
student, hence his interest in the Roman
remains we've unearthed. Hughes, on the
other hand, is quite brilliant. He's one of
my history students, but I suspect his real
interest is my daughter, who is a bit of a
hoyden, I'm afraid . . . '

My thoughts turned to my own family.
I'd neglected them to the point where the
distance between us seemed impossible to
bridge. When my son, Albert, died of
consumption, I hadn't shed a single tear.
I don't know why, I just did not have it in
me. Emma pleaded with me to take a rest
from work. But there was always an
excuse: the Fenians, the anti-czarists, the
Jubilee Plot. Albert died four years ago,
and I hadn't taken a single leave of
absence since. It had taken an order from
the assistant commissioner himself two

days ago, and even then I'd followed it to the letter, ignoring the intent: *get out of London*.

I did: on the trail of the Macedonian.

As we entered Wilmington village, ruins loomed up ahead, behind a high stone wall.

'I say, do you know that it was very near here that the scientific study of archaeology began?' asked Edford.

I bit back a harsh reply, and tried to sound interested. 'No, I didn't.'

'Cissbury Knot. It was General Pitt-Rivers' first major dig — that's Wilmington Priory over there. The foundations are eleventh century, but the ruins are fourteenth. We'll cut along in front, next to the coppice. Now, I was saying about General Pitt-Rivers; he started . . . '

We turned onto a narrow footpath between the priory and a small, but dense wood. Moss and the tendrils of larger plants encroached on the path. The wall was covered with lichen and creeping ivy, their roots eating away at the stone, as if Nature was trying to reclaim the building and return the Earth to its primeval state.

I glanced at the dank, fecund wood, and shuddered involuntarily.

Edford crooked his stick under his arm and enumerated on his fingertips. ' . . . One, stratigraphic excavation, meaning layer by layer; two, the significance of the small find and the plain artefact; three, the use of field notes, photography, and plan maps; four, the publication of results; and five, the cooperation of indigenous populations.'

'It sounds exactly like detective work,' I mused, darting another look at the eldritch trees.

'I say, Langham, what was that?'

I realised my blunder — my first ever — too late. 'I may as well tell you the truth. I'm a police detective, an inspector at Scotland Yard.'

'It's *Signore* Rossi, isn't it? I knew it! He's a socialist! Or a communist — no, an anarchist — he's an anarchist, isn't he?'

Although I usually err on the side of discretion, I thought it prudent to assuage at least a little of Edford's curiosity. 'I've no interest in Rossi, it's Makedonski I'm watching.'

'The Russian? Is he an anarchist?'

'He's Macedonian, and no, he's not an anarchist. It's more of a routine observation.'

He gave me an exaggerated wink, and pressed a finger to his lips. 'You can't fool me, Inspector, but don't concern yourself. I'm as loyal a subject as any; you may rest assured that no one shall learn your secret from me.'

It wasn't his politics, but his habitual chattering I feared. Despite my gaffe, I felt relieved when we passed the edge of the wood, out onto a sward. The feeling was short-lived, however, and I grew uneasy again as we approached a line of massive oaks. Edford pointed over the tops of the trees to a steep hill. In the moonlight I discerned the outline of a huge man in a sickly, sulphurous colour. I gasped. 'Is that him?'

'The Long Man, guardian of the South Downs. He is two hundred and thirty-feet high, but he's faded away the last few millennia, so the local folk marked him out with bricks. Come along, I'll show you our dig.'

Edford strode in between the last two

oaks, but I walked around instead, joining him at the foot of the hill. The row of trees extended away to our left. Immediately in front of them a curious garden consisting of alternating rectangular holes and semicircular piles of loose earth had been dug. Very close to one of the oaks, a canvas sheet was secured to the ground with pegs.

'There you have it. Half a dozen separate excavations so far, and every one of them has yielded human remains.' He produced his pipe, and a tobacco pouch. 'But that one there,' he gestured towards the cover, 'is a rare find. A complete skeleton. We're taking our time with old Scipio, in order to keep his mortal remains intact . . . '

Edford's voice faded into the background as I looked from the giant to the trees and then back to the giant. A feeling of dread, or perhaps a wave of exhaustion, overwhelmed me — I saw a flash of movement on the periphery of my vision and spun towards the nearest oak, raising my penang-lawyer and reaching inside my coat.

'I say, old fellow, are you alright?'

'Oh, yes, quite. I saw something move — in the tree — it startled me, that's all.'

'Indeed. You do seem a little on edge. I'm not surprised with all those anarchists trying to kill Her Majesty. Now join me in a pipe and I'll tell you all about the Wilmington Giant . . .'

He proceeded to do exactly that, expounding his theory that the figure was originally a Wicker Man, used by the Druids to sacrifice captured Roman soldiers. It was horrible thought, made worse by the fact that there was much evidence to support it. I couldn't help feeling sorry for the Romans, even if they were invaders. When we returned to the inn, I knew I would dream of screaming, burning men — if I slept at all.

★ ★ ★

Makedonski and I breakfasted alone on saturday. As soon as he was finished, he excused himself and returned to his room. I spent the rest of the morning smoking and reading the papers in the parlour. Makedonski didn't come down, but four visitors were sent up.

The first was a very large Russian, with a horribly scarred face, whom I recognised as Nevskaja. He and Makedonski had served under Karastoilov in Kresna in seventy-eight. I was surprised to see him, because we had no record of his being in the country. He did not stay long. The second visitor was obviously a sailor from his dress, gait, and speech. A merchant captain from Glasgow, I deduced. He left after a lengthy interview. I waited twenty minutes, and was about to rise when another two men arrived and asked for Makedonski. I picked my paper back up, and watched and listened as inconspicuously as I was able.

The man who addressed Rossi was about my own height, but much leaner, with a prominent nose and chin. His companion was shorter, with an athletic frame, and a slight limp. Rossi sent one of the boys up with the taller gentleman's card, and I was given time to refine my observations. The shorter man was a former Army officer; the handkerchief in his sleeve, his bearing, and his moustache bespoke as much. I was unable to determine his current employment without making my interest obvious, so I returned to his companion.

A cold chill ran down my spine: the man was scrutinising me — with a skill at least equal to my own. He knew I was watching him, and he knew that I knew I was being watched. His fingers were long and delicate, the hands stained with chemicals. His movements betrayed the controlled energy of a sportsman, but he was obviously a man of some intellect. His employment was also a mystery to me, but I decided he counted music and fencing among his interests. I wondered what he would make of my puffy eyes and weary mien.

The Chemist and the Soldier left a quarter of an hour later. I waited a further fifteen minutes, and when Makedonski had still not appeared, approached Rossi.

'*Buon pomeriggio, Signore* Langham. You have had a restful morning, I trust?'

'Yes, thank you, I have. I'd like my buggy, please, I'm driving out this afternoon.'

'*Si, Signore.*' He shouted for the stable boy, and gave the necessary orders.

'It was very quiet at breakfast. I thought you said you were full last night?' I asked casually.

'*Si, si,* we are. We have only six rooms, *Signore. Signore* Makedonski has taken two, one for a sitting-room. The other three rooms are taken by Professor Edford and the two young gentlemen. They leave very early in the morning, and I prepare them the cold luncheon. They are digging for the treasure in Wilmington.'

'Yes, we walked over last night.'

'And *Signore* Makedonski, I see why he has taken the two rooms. He has had four visitors already this morning.'

'Has he? I didn't notice.'

My buggy arrived and I thanked Rossi, tipped the boy, and set off for Newhaven. I'd decided that Makedonski was in Sussex for business rather than pleasure long before his meetings. The ship's captain could, of course, have travelled from anywhere, but the nearest ports were Newhaven and Shoreham. Newhaven's harbour was the smaller

33

of the two — and the less likely — but I recalled seeing a barque docked there yesterday evening, when I'd hired the buggy. The *Lilian Younger* was still in the same place when I arrived, and I took a drive around the port before lunching at the Dolphin.

I was favoured with good fortune at the public house, for I found not only an ideal seat from which to observe the barque, but also a publican much given to gossip. For the price of my custom and a few compliments, I was told more than I wanted to know about life in Newhaven. Of interest, however, was the following: the Glaswegian sailor was Joseph Munro, captain of the *Lilian Younger*; the barque was due to set sail for Shanghai via Bremen and Le Havre tomorrow; and the crew were very reticent about their cargo, which hadn't arrived yet.

I supped mug after mug of ale, praying I would sleep peacefully later. Several sailors left and returned to the barque, but nothing out of the ordinary occurred until early evening, when a loafer shared some of his tobacco with the crewman on duty at the gangplank. I lifted my field-glass for a better look and noted that the man bore a faint resemblance to the Chemist. The deception would have fooled most, but I'd become something of an expert in the use of disguises myself during the Fenian bombings. The Chemist smoked and talked with the hand for about half an hour before sidling off in the direction of the high street. I added the likelihood that he had trained as an actor to my mental docket.

I was starting to feel drowsy from the alcohol. I considered following the Chemist, but decided against it and walked up Castle Hill, enjoying the sea breeze as I climbed past the new fort. I toured the summit, and found a vantage point from where I could maintain my vigil. My persistence was rewarded when, shortly after eight, Nevskaja — the Russian — boarded. An hour and a quarter later, with the sun setting, I reclaimed my buggy and returned to Alfriston.

I arrived to find Rossi waiting up for me. His night porter had reported for duty drunk, and Rossi had sent him home. He locked up behind me, told me he'd left a cold platter on the sideboard, and bade me goodnight. I was grateful for the supper, especially when I found it accompanied by another decanter of armagnac. I took the food and drink up to my room, and gave full reign to both my appetites. The last thing I remember was lying on the bed and looking at the clock.

It was an hour before midnight.

★ ★ ★

I woke with an unpleasant start, and an inexplicable fear. Something was wrong. I rubbed the sleep from my eyes and was immediately reminded of the Lushai Hills. Why the memory should come at such a time, I had no idea. I looked at the clock and cursed: it was already after nine. I cursed Rossi for not sending the maid up with my hot water, cursed myself for drinking half the brandy and bolting my door, and then Rossi again when I found my boots still filthy. I performed a hasty and perfunctory toilet, during which the combination of my unsteady hand and the cold water caused me to slice open my chin.

I stormed downstairs to find Rossi with a police constable. 'What the hell's going on?' I demanded.

'*Scusi, Signore* Langham, *buon* — '

'It's not *buon* anything. I've overslept, there was no hot water, and my boots haven't even been cleaned!'

'A million apologies, *Signore*, but your door was locked and the girl did not want to — '

'Excuse me, sir, would you be a guest at this inn?' said the constable.

'Of course I'm a bloody guest here,' I snapped.

'Now then, milord, I'll ask you to mind — '

I whipped out my warrant card. 'Chief Inspector Langham, Scotland Yard. State your business.'

He squinted at the card, took a few seconds to absorb the information, and saluted. 'My apologies, sir, I'm Constable Hampton, East Sussex Constabulary.' I nodded and he continued. 'One of Mr

Rossi's lodgers were murdered last night, sir. Professor Edford. He were shot to death in Wilmington. Inspector Brown come down from Lewes. He sent me to — '

'Mr Rossi, my buggy — and quickly. Constable, pay attention. First, I want you to make sure that none of the other three guests leave the inn. Professor Edford has two of his students with him, Parker and Hughes,' Rossi opened his mouth, but I cut him off, 'There's also a foreign gentleman by the name of Makedonski. I'll be questioning all three of them when I get back. If any one of them does try to leave, you have my permission to take him into custody forthwith.'

'Mr Rossi just told me that Parker's already left, sir.'

'What?'

'*Si, si, Signore.* The boy from Wilmington came here first. I sent him for *Signore* Hampton and I went to get *Dottore* Roundtree myself. When I come back, *Signore* Parker had taken a carriage and gone.'

'If you ask me, you gentlemen from the police force should be looking for Parker. He bolted as soon as we heard about the professor.' Hughes had joined us.

'I do not require your advice, Mr Hughes, but I do require your evidence. Tell me what happened.'

'He was cool as anything at first, but then the boy came back and spoke to him. I was on my way to the kitchen to try and find somebody to brew the coffee. When I got back to the parlour, Parker was as white as a sheet. He mumbled something about leaving and dashed off to the stables.'

'Where's the body?' I asked Hampton.

'Where they was doing their digging, sir, under the Long Man.'

'You have your orders. I'll be back directly.'

I left my buggy outside the priory, and took the overgrown footpath. I had a sense of *déjà vu* and, even in the clear light of day, felt a minatory force emanating from the Sylvan demesne. I quickened my step, leaving the wood behind and crossing the sward. A uniformed policeman and three other men were standing at the foot of Windover Hill, a short distance from the last oak. As I came closer I saw Edford's body lying in the exact place where he and I had stood and smoked on Friday night. The Chemist, bent double, was scuttling round his corpse like an enormous insect. The image was repellent, and I averted my gaze.

I was able to determine the identities of all three of the men in civilian dress before I reached them: Inspector Brown, Dr Roundtree, and the Soldier, whom I could now see was also a doctor. 'Inspector Brown? I'm Chief Inspector Langham, from Scotland Yard.'

'Good morning, sir. The Yard? That was quick.'

'I've been in Alfriston since Friday evening, at the Star Inn.'

'The Star! You knew — '

'I met him on Friday night. I've told your man Hampton to make sure the other lodgers await our return. Now perhaps you'll tell me who the gentleman examining the scene of the murder is, and what you know about the crime thus far.'

'Yes, sir. The energetic gentleman is Mr Sherlock Holmes. He and Dr Watson,' he indicated the Soldier, 'happened to be in Lewes, so I took the liberty of requesting their assistance. This is Dr Roundtree, from Alfriston.'

I acknowledged the doctors and asked Brown, 'Mr Sherlock Holmes of Baker Street?'

'Yes, sir. You've heard of him?'

'My colleague Inspector Gregson holds him in very high esteem.'

'Mr Holmes asked me and the doctors to keep back while he made his search. He's already recovered the bullet from one of the trees.' Brown unwrapped his pocket handkerchief, and showed me a flattened piece of lead.

'The projectile is complete,' said Watson. 'Quite remarkable when you consider it entered and exited the professor's skull before coming to rest in the tree trunk. My guess is point four-four-two calibre.'

'Army Medical Department?' I asked him.

'Yes, I served with the Berkshires.' He smiled.

I indicated his leg. 'Maiwand?'

'I had that misfortune. You are also an old campaigner; British Army or Indian?'

'Indian, the Sirmoor Rifles. If your appraisal of the bullet is correct then the weapon was very likely a Webley Royal Irish Constabulary Model. It's the most popular of the point four-four-two cartridge loaders.'

'Because it fires double-action,' said Watson

'Precisely.'

'And I should think you are wearing the exact model on your person underneath your left arm, Chief Inspector Langham,' said Sherlock Holmes.

I was taken aback. I am never without the Webley, but it usually passes undetected because of my height, breadth of shoulder, and tailored coat. What disturbed me even more was that Holmes had been too far away to hear me introduce myself.

His face was flushed, his brows drawn, and now that we were at close quarters, I could see a steely glitter in his eyes. 'You are most perceptive, sir.'

He turned to the inspector. 'Thank you, Brown, my researches here are complete. If you will be so good as to allow the doctors to examine the body?' Brown, Watson, and Roundtree left us. Holmes extended his hand. 'I am Sherlock Holmes, consulting detective by profession. I believe your business in Alfriston concerns Mr Nikulica Makedonski.'

My jaw dropped open as he took my hand in an iron grip. 'I . . . I see Gregson did not over-estimate your skills.'

'Gregson? He is the smartest of the Yarders, although I confess I have not met all of the official force.'

'How do you know about Makedonski? And my own identity?'

'My brother is employed by the Home Office. He has alluded to a Chief Inspector Langham as the head of the Special Irish Branch upon several occasions, remarking that the man resembles his name.'

'My name?'

'Langham is derived from long, meaning tall. You are certainly a long man. Of late, Section D has turned its attention to Continental anarchists and it can hardly be coincidence that I saw you in the parlour of the inn where Makedonski, the Macedonian nationalist, has taken lodgings.'

'In that case, may I ask what you were doing visiting Makedonski and subsequently disguising yourself as a dockyard loafer in Newhaven?'

He chuckled. 'A touch Langham, an undeniable touch! I suggest that after we hear what the doctors have to say, we compare notes. I have no doubt each will supplement the other. In the mean time I'll tell you one thing which may help you in the case — if you would care to hear it?'

I was disappointed that Holmes' energies had yielded only a single point. Nor had his knowledge of my identity and purpose seemed clever once explained. I wondered if Gregson hadn't embellished his tales of the criminal agent's prowess. 'Certainly, Mr Holmes.'

'The murderer is just under six feet high, blonde, wore badly worn boots of a size ten, and is an expert marksman. He was also no stranger to Edford, and arrived here some time after the professor.'

I was once again astonished. 'How could you possibly deduce all of that?'

'Excellent, Langham! You have answered your own question: the science of deduction. I have applied my methods to the scene of the crime, but they are equally effective when put to other uses. In reading your own book of life, for example.'

'My book of life?'

'It is impossible to deceive one trained in observation and analysis. Thus I can say with confidence that you served with a Goorkha regiment in India, suffer from chronic sleeplessness, remonstrated with your landlord before leaving the Star, and have recently been engaged in the protection of the Queen.'

'You do not need me to tell you that you are correct on all counts, Mr Holmes. As for your description of the murderer, Parker — the missing student — is five feet eleven inches in height, fair-haired, and wears a size ten boot. And I'm sure he's had plenty of opportunity to learn to shoot at Melford Hall.'

'He is missing? Well, well, let us see if the doctors can throw any fresh light upon this matter.'

Roundtree addressed me. 'Dr Watson and I are both of the opinion that Professor Edford was killed between ten and two o'clock of last night. Inspector Brown has confirmed that Edford was in the habit of taking exercise before he retired for the night.'

'He was,' I said to Holmes. 'He also suffered from insomnia.'

'Thank you, Doctor,' said Brown before turning to me. 'Will you be taking over the investigation, sir?'

'No, Brown, the case is yours, but I should like to satisfy myself that the assassination was not a political one.'

'You assistance would be most welcome, sir.'

'Very good. If you and Dr Roundtree make the necessary arrangements here, perhaps Mr Holmes and Dr Watson will accompany me back to the Star?'

As I rode back with Holmes and Watson, I spoke plainly of my indiscretion on Friday night. It was possible that either Edford's loquaciousness or his curiosity had put Makedonski, or even Rossi, on their guard. While Makedonski and Rossi were short and dark, Nevskaja matched Holmes' description, and could have done the Macedonian's work for him. In return Holmes informed me that he had been engaged by Lloyds to investigate an insurance fraud, and believed the *Lilian Younger* of Panama to be the *Sophy Anderson* of Clydebank, reported lost with all hands off the coast of the Outer Hebrides three years ago.

On our return to the inn, we found Hampton in command, with Makedonski and Hughes awaiting us impatiently. Holmes went up to examine Edford's room, and I questioned Rossi.

'After you came back last night, *Signore*, I lock both doors. I leave the key to the back door on the peg, but I give *Signore* Edford the front door key because he say he want to go out for his walk before he goes to sleep. I hear him open and close the door half an hour before midnight, but I am asleep before he comes back. One of the maids says she hears a gentleman leaving by the back door at midnight. This morning, I find the back door is locked and the key is in place. The front door is also locked, but there is no key.'

'Did you or any of the servants hear anyone return in the night?'

'*No, no, Signore.*'

I joined Holmes and Watson upstairs. Until we discovered evidence to the contrary, it appeared that Edford had gone out for his usual ramble at half-past eleven. Makedonski, Parker, or Hughes had left the inn half an hour later. Had they left to follow the professor, or for another reason altogether?

'I have found nothing of interest,' said Holmes. 'I should like to speak with Makedonski.'

Makedonski was waiting in his sitting room. 'So, you are not Langham the stockbroker, you are Langham the secret policeman. Am I right?'

'I'm Chief Inspector Langham of Scotland Yard. You have already met Mr Holmes and Dr Watson, so I'll proceed with our business. What, exactly are you doing in a country inn on the South Downs?'

Makedonski took a silver case from his inside pocket, removed a Turkish cigarette, and lit it with a match. He smiled as he exhaled. The acrid smell of the smoke reminded me of waking this morning. 'I did not kill Professor Edford. I came back to my room after supper, and I did not leave it until I went down to Rossi's excuse for breakfast this morning.'

'You haven't answered my question.'

He smiled again, full of contempt. 'I am taking the country air for my health.'

'No, you're not.'

'I think you will find that Mr Makedonski is organising an armed expedition,' said Holmes. 'When I asked you where the *Lilian Younger* was bound yesterday, what did you tell me?'

Makedonski said nothing and Holmes repeated the question. The Macedonian drew heavily on his cigarette. 'You remember as well as I do.'

'Yes, I do. Hong Kong via Bremen and Le Havre. And yet Captain Munro told his crew they are destined for Shanghai. You would do well to pay attention to detail. The barque is in fact bound for Macedonia, is it not?'

Makedonski shrugged. 'Have I committed any crime in this matter?'

'I believe you are innocent of the fact that the *Lilian Younger* is the *Sophy Anderson*. Did you leave your room at all last night?'

'No, I did not.'

'Did you hear anyone else leave?'

'No.'

'I very much doubt you had anything to do with Professor Edford's death. It would be extremely foolish to murder a hapless archaeologist while plotting another uprising, would it not?'

Makedonski said nothing.

'What are you doing in Alfriston?' I asked again.

'I am financing a trading expedition, Inspector. I was not aware of any subterfuge regarding the *Lilian Younger*. If you allow me to do so, my associate Mr Nevskaja — whom you will also have recognised yesterday — and I will sail from your shores tomorrow afternoon.' He tossed his cigarette end onto the floor. 'Never to return, I hope.'

'You will have to use another barque to transport your arms and ammunition,' I said.

'Quite so,' said Holmes. 'The *Lilian Younger* was impounded this morning and Captain Munro placed under arrest.'

The Macedonian swore between his teeth.

I asked Makedonski about the previous night, but his answers remained unchanged. I made a note of his London address, which I already knew, and informed him he was free to leave. Holmes and Watson left for Newhaven, and Brown arrived shortly after. We commenced our interrogation of Hughes, *Signore* and *Signora* Rossi, and their staff — including the now sober night porter. It was a dull and disappointing process, which yielded nothing new. Makedonski left before we'd finished, and Hughes directly after.

Brown returned to Wilmington to take charge of the local inquiries, and I found myself alone in the parlour.

I tried unsuccessfully to relax. Despite my first good night's sleep in weeks — no, months — my nerves were still in shreds. I was about to call for a brandy, but decided on a pot of coffee instead. It was probably yesterday's over-indulgence that left me feeling so wretched. Before I could summon him, Rossi appeared with a scruffy youth of about eleven.

'*Mi Scusi, Signore, Signore* Hampton has sent this boy to you.'

'Thank you, Mr Rossi. What's your name, lad?'

'Sid, sir.'

'Sit down, Sid. You've done a very responsible job today, well done.'

'Thank you, sir.'

'Where did you come from this morning?'

'The Priory House in Wilmington, sir. That's where I lives and works, isn't it?'

'You must have been up early this morning?'

'Yessir, I were.'

'And the master of the house sent you to fetch Constable Hampton and Doctor Roundtree?'

He nodded vigorously. 'Yessir — I mean nossir — it were the lady.'

'You came here first?'

'Yessir. I weren't too sure where to find Mr Hampton and I knows Mr Rossi is always up bright and early. Also, I had the telegram for Mr Parker.'

'You had a message for Mr Parker?' I asked.

'Yessir, I did. It was Mrs Wright as gave it me. Only I forgot. But then I remembered and after I found the doctor, I brought it back. I couldn't find Mr Rossi, but there was a gent in here. When I asked him if he knew where Mr Parker of Melford Hall was, he said it were him, so I gave him the telegram. Did I do right, sir?'

'Quite right. Did you see what was in the telegram?'

'No, sir.'

'Did the gentleman say anything to you?'

He shook his head. 'Nossir. He just

said thank you and I hopped it back to the Priory.'

I tossed him a shilling. 'That's for your trouble, Sid, now off you go.'

He caught the coin, touched his cap, and disappeared.

Had Parker's flight been nothing to do with Edford? I wanted to think without interruption, so I asked the maid to bring the coffee up to my room. I considered Holmes' description of the murderer. Parker and Nevskaja were both possibilities, but Holmes had said that Edford knew his killer. That left only Parker. Either Parker or someone else, perhaps someone from Wilmington or even Oxford. Parker's sudden departure may have been because of the telegram. Similarly, the fact that someone had left the inn last night may also have had nothing to with Edford. Many a policeman has drawn an erroneous conclusion from mere coincidence.

And yet . . .

★ ★ ★

'Chief Inspector, are you in there!'

'Hold on, man!' I lay slumped in my chair while someone hammered at the door. 'Who is it?'

'Brown, sir. Mr Holmes would like to see us at Wilmington.'

It was half-past seven. I glanced at the mirror and was shocked by what I saw. My eyes had large, dark circles under them, my chin was caked in dried blood, and scores of yellow bristles had survived the cold blade. I was pale and drawn, in dire need of more rest.

I would take a holiday — but only after I'd solved Edford's murder.

'There you are, sir. Mr Holmes asked us to meet him at Windover Hill. I was going to suggest a walk, but you look all done in. We can take the trap — '

'No, let's walk.'

As we were leaving the inn, Rossi attracted my attention with a polite cough. '*Mi Scusi, Signore. Signore* Brown say that my front door key was found with the professor. I was hoping if I may have it back soon?'

'Brown?'

'I don't see any problem with that, sir, unless you've any objection?'

'No, of course not.'

'*Gratzi infinite, Signore*. And once again, my apologies for this morning; the maid — '

'Don't worry about it,' I interrupted.

'And your boots, *Signore*, I sent the stable boy up to clean them at eleven o'clock last night. He says he did, but I have docked his pay . . . '

We left and I pressed Brown for news. Sir Roger Parker of Melford Hall had died yesterday. A courier was sent to Wilmington in error, arriving late last night, and this was the news the boy had delivered this morning. It didn't eliminate Parker as a suspect, but it certainly explained his actions. We lapsed into silence as we walked up Wilmington Street, and I considered Holmes' description of the murderer again. Five foot ten or eleven inches tall, with fair hair, and an experienced shootist. He may have used a Webley revolver, wore much-used boots of a size ten . . .

Boots.

What had Rossi said about the stable boy?

The weather had taken a turn for the worse and the Long Man's peculiar square head was shrouded in mist. Holmes and Watson stood next to the end oak, motionless, like two prehistoric sentinels. I remembered rubbing the sleep from my eyes this morning, and I knew why I'd thought of Assam. My mind raced and my heart pounded. Was Holmes always right? Not this time. This time he was wrong, I knew it.

The murderer was over six feet, not under.

'Good evening, gentlemen,' he said. 'Before we discuss the results of my investigation, I'd like to have a look at your revolver, Langham. You wouldn't object if I dry-fired it, would you? I should like to test Watson's assertion of the superiority of the double-action mechanism.'

I hesitated for a second, then withdrew the Webley, and offered it to him butt-first.

'Thank you.' He broke open the

breech, examined the cylinder, and ejected the five rounds. He handed them to Watson and sniffed the Webley. 'This revolver has been cleaned recently. Very recently.'

'You were wrong, Holmes,' I said.

'In which respect?' He closed the revolver.

'The murderer is over six feet tall, your own height actually.'

'You are quite correct. I deduced from the length of the man's stride that he was less than six feet in height. In nine cases out of ten, I should have been correct, but I did not take into account that the gentleman in question is in very poor health, and that his weakness reproduced the signs of a shorter man.'

I looked into his sharp, piercing eyes, exactly level with my own.

'Dr Watson is of the opinion that you were not aware of your actions. I may have fallen into error over the height of the murderer, but you could not have deceived me had you known. Therefore, you did not know, and I can confirm the good doctor's diagnosis. Nonetheless, I took the precaution of disarming you.'

'Mr Holmes, this is outrageous! Chief Inspector Langham is a — '

'No, Brown, Holmes is right. I don't remember anything, but it must have been me. It could only have been me.'

'When did you reach that conclusion?' asked Holmes.

'As I walked over. My final memory of last night is an hour before midnight. This morning I woke late, and when I rubbed my eyes I was reminded of skirmishing in the Lushai Hills. Because my right hand smelled of gunpowder. After I — after I — found Edford, I must have returned to my room, bolted the door, and cleaned my revolver . . . '

'But not your hands,' said Holmes.

'No.'

Brown protested, 'But, sir! Doctor, surely this . . . '

'I have heard of similar cases,' said Watson. 'The alienists call it dementia. I'm afraid I noted the symptoms in the chief inspector as soon as we met.'

'I returned from Assam with my vision slightly impaired, an ague, and a hatred of cats. I was convinced there was something else too, but I had no idea . . . '

'I'm sorry Brown, Mr Holmes is right,' said Watson.

Brown sighed and said, 'Are you sure, sir?'

'Yes.' I looked up at the Long Man, his head in the clouds. 'And you'd better put the derbies on, just in case.'

Author's Note: As with so many improbable tales, this one is based on historical fact. While Roderick Langham investigated his last case, the top thief-taker in the *Sûreté*, Inspector Robert Ledru, became the first recorded 'homicidal somnambulist', across the channel in Le Havre. Ledru had to solve the murder himself — which, to his credit, he did — and his schizophrenia was caused by syphilis rather than toxoplasmosis.

Fleet

Professor Goodspeed — Anniversary Chair in Archaeology, University of York — ran his hands over the package on his desk with undisguised glee. Inside, beneath the layers of plastic and cardboard, were the spoils of his larceny — depending upon one's definition of the term. He didn't much care about terminology today. Gradually, he became aware that the persistent ringing was his telephone. He lifted the receiver without averting his gaze. 'Goodspeed.'

'Matt, it's me, where are my chapters?'

Goodspeed had no desire to speak to his agent. 'In my head.'

'That's not what I want to hear. I had a conference call with Hodder this morning. If the third book doesn't sell as well as *The Templar Ascendancy*, they won't be renewing your contract. Do I have to remind you how badly *Knight's Bane* flopped?'

'*Bane* was a much better novel than *Ascendancy*. It flopped because of the marketing. Hodder's fault, not mine.'

'*Ascendancy* sold off the back of *The Da Vinci Code*. Nobody wanted to know about knights dying of leprosy. I told you we were taking a big risk. Readers wanted Knights Templar, not Knights of bloody Saint Lawrence.'

'Saint Lazarus, Knights of bloody Saint Lazarus.'

'Lazarus, Lawrence, that's exactly what I mean. The deadline is four months away.'

'I wrote *Ascendancy* in four.'

'I know, but I need to be more involved, take a proper look. We can't afford to fail this time. Tell me you're going to start writing tonight.'

Goodspeed stroked the parcel again. It was postmarked 'Lincoln' and stamped 'Royal Mail Sameday' and 'Fragile'. 'I'm going to start tonight.'

'Really!'

'Yes, really. The book will be finished in three months and you'll have your three chapters by the weekend.'

'You've no idea how relieved I am. Seeing as you haven't started yet, do you think you could bring back Christopher de Belleby in this one?'

Goodspeed sighed, wondering if his agent had actually read either of his novels. 'I know they're billed as thrillers, but don't you think that would be stretching my credibility just a little? *Ascendancy* ended with de Belleby in irons, descending to the seabed with a Saracen under each arm.'

'But you didn't actually say he drowned.'

'I'm not resurrecting de Belleby, but you can tell Hodder it will be another Templar novel.'

'Thank God for that! I'm going to ring them right now. Is there anything else you can give me? You know, concept, blurb, anything?'

'It's going to start on Friday the 13th of October, 1307.' Goodspeed read the label on the parcel: 'Conservation Restoration, County Council Heritage Service'. He smiled to himself. 'And the title is *Fleet*.'

'I like it already.'

'You're not going to like *Fleet*, you're

going to love it. Because it's going to make you rich. Very rich. Goodbye.'

★ ★ ★

At midnight, alone in his study, Goodspeed inspected the Oliphant. Although the ivory hunting horn was made from an elephant's tusk, it wasn't as big as he remembered. Even without the curve it would only extend from elbow to fingertip, and he was a small man. He put on his reading glasses, lifted the artefact, and examined it more closely. The restorers had done a remarkable job. He ran his index finger lightly along the place where the crack had been, and could feel only the slightest of indentations. They'd also cleaned it. He could see the marks where the rings had been fixed for attaching a strap, and even the detail of the circular motifs, each depicting a different battle scene. Worth every penny, even though he'd used his own money.

It was clean enough to put to his lips.

Goodspeed spent another minute looking at the Oliphant from different angles, then placed it back on the pile of books. He turned to his laptop, created a new document, and titled it 'Fleet'. Not that money was a problem once he'd realised he could make use of the same research twice: once for his academic work, and once for his popular fiction. That way the university funded his novels and paid his salary. *Fleet* would be based on the Temple Garth dig.

Goodspeed had spent most of the spring excavating the ruins of the Templar Preceptory of Faxfleet. There was almost nothing left above ground, but in the early fourteenth century it had been the most prosperous of the Templars' ten Yorkshire strongholds. 'Fax' meant horse, and 'fleet', river. The name came from the preceptory's position at the confluence of two of England's most important rivers, the Trent and the Humber. Goodspeed had been digging at what was known as the Water Gate — although it was now far from the riverbank — when he'd found the Oliphant.

He'd been alone when he'd spotted the grubby sliver of ivory, the students all working on the foundations of the church. At the very same instant he'd recognised a hunting horn, he'd had the flash of inspiration. Title, characters, plot — everything at once. Dawn, Friday the 13th of October, 1307. King Phillip's men arrest eighteen hundred Templar knights. Few French Templars escape his dragnet, with the significant exception of Gérard de Villiers, Preceptor of France. When the king's servants descend on La Rochelle, they find the Templar fleet — eighteen galleys, and an unspecified number of men and horses — gone. Legend had it they'd sailed to the Orkneys, and thence to Rhode Island, in America. De Villiers would be his protagonist, removing the missing treasure from the Paris Temple, fleeing to La Rochelle, and escaping with the help of a magic Oliphant.

Goodspeed hadn't consciously decided to hide the horn in his bag, he'd just done it without thinking. In his expert opinion, it pre-dated the Templars, and most likely had nothing to do with the preceptory anyway. It was probably from the Anglo-Saxon period, although not from these shores. Frankish, perhaps. He had another creative epiphany and picked it up again. The Oliphant in *Fleet* would be the horn from *La Chanson de Roland*. Roland, the favourite of Charlemagne, the paladin who perished at the Battle of Roncevaux Pass. That would add a bit of interest for the history buffs — if there were any amongst his readers. Goodspeed chuckled. This novel was practically going to write itself.

The restoration went against the grain of his academic training, but the texture of the smooth contours beneath his caress was all the justification he required. He traced a finger from bell to tip and considered his real motive.

With the crack mended, it might actually work.

Although there was no metal mouth-piece, Goodspeed raised the Oliphant. The ivory was cool and made his lips tingle. He didn't know quite what to do — or what would happen — so he interrupted his experiment, rose from his desk, and opened the window. He looked out at the firmament, illuminated by the weak glow of a three-quarter moon half-covered by a solitary cloud. He leant out the window, inhaled deeply, and blew — hard.

The noise was not unlike a hooter.

Goodspeed felt rather foolish, but at the same time mentally and physically invigorated by the sound he had produced with his own breath.

He inhaled again, drawing the air deep into his lungs — the door flew open. 'What on earth do you think you're doing at this hour!' His wife.

Above, the moon beamed brighter, no longer obscured by the cloud, and he imagined he had blown it away.

★   ★   ★

Next day Goodspeed worked everything out. The first part of the novel would be set in Paris — he could use the research he'd done for *Ascendancy* — and the second in Faxfleet itself, where de Villiers would lose his Oliphant. *Fleet* would finish in the Orkneys. Goodspeed could spend August in Stromness or Kirkwall,

68

and do some on location research as he wrote. He glanced at his watch for the umpteenth time that afternoon. Ten to seven. Outside, the sun was still shining.

Perfect.

He picked up his sling bag, locked his office, and left the Centre for Medieval Studies. He entered the Museum Gardens, passed the museum itself, and took the footpath through the ruins of St Mary's Abbey. At the timber-framed Hospitium, he turned right, walking up a gentle grassy bank which brought him to a mound at the north-west corner of the park.

Goodspeed could see the River Ouse over the walls, and the Yorkshire Wheel beyond. He looked back: other than a couple weaving their way towards St Mary's, he was alone. The bells of the Minster chimed. Seven o'clock in the evening was his favourite time of day or night in York. There was about half an hour of cross-over, when the city was all but deserted in between the departure of the workers and the arrival of the revellers. He ran his hand through his thinning hair, enjoying the cat's-paw coming from the river.

As soon as the bells ceased, Goodspeed reached for the Oliphant.

This time the ivory felt almost alive to the fondle of his fingers. He shivered with anticipation as he took a deep breath and inflated his lungs. He put the horn to his lips and exhaled. He didn't even register the sound for all the sensations racing through his mind and body. He felt light-headed, dizzy, slightly disorientated; then he was seized by a sudden, delicious, furious energy. He blew again, relishing the blare. He filled his lungs a third time, stretching his skinny chest to full capacity, and let loose once more.

The white cotton-wool cumulus cloud above the Ferris Wheel jumped to the right.

Goodspeed knew it was coincidence. Pure power coursed through his veins. He felt a drop of perspiration trickle down his spine, filled his lungs until he feared they would burst, and trumpeted again.

Two clouds sailed rapidly over the Wheel, moving north.

The wind was blowing from across the Ouse, from the west.

Goodspeed coughed, spluttered, and sucked down more air. His eyes watered and his temples throbbed. Again he blew, sweat breaking out on his forehead. An unruly clump of cumulus, unimpressed by his efforts thus far, contorted as if it too were drawing breath. A little finger of funnel-cloud appeared below it. A tiny whirlwind, a little twister of his own making. Goodspeed found a halting rhythm, heaving, huffing, and puffing as he blasted.

Each time he sounded the horn the vortex flexed and contracted, and each time it moved a little closer towards him. One more flurry and it would reach the river. There was a team of rowers exercising and he wanted to see what would happen when his personal tornado touched them. Gasping and panting, he rested his elbows on his knees. He bloated his chest, stood erect, lifted the Oliphant —

'Oi, leave it out!' The park warden. Goodspeed couldn't speak, his lips were numb. 'Anymore of that, and I'll have you for disturbing the peace.'

To the east a dense, black bank of cumulonimbus hovered high above the Minster.

★   ★   ★

It had taken Goodspeed two days to shake the commitments of work and family for an afternoon on his own. Instead of beginning the novel, he'd driven to Faxfleet at once. He found himself at the Water Gate, facing the Humber across a flat expanse of flood-plain. He could see for miles in each direction, and although there were a few buildings scattered in the vista, they were the only signs of life. Finally, no one to interrupt him. He'd been thinking about how to improve his performance. Clearly, he was not built for such an instrument, nor did he have the time to increase his lung capacity through exercise. Instead, he must try to curb his enthusiasm, and take three or four seconds in between each blast so he could maintain a continuous resonance.

Goodspeed held the Oliphant loose at

his side and prepared his chest for the exertion to come by drawing progressively deeper breaths. To the south, across the water, he could see as far as the horizon, the overarching sky forming a massive amphitheatre for his benefit. It was full of cloud, three layers suspended in the atmosphere: stratos, altus, and cirrus. Some were white, some grey, some a dirty brown.

Perfect.

He would make them all dance to his call.

Goodspeed raised the elephant's tusk and began.

A puff of cumulus hopped in the familiar elemental knee-jerk. He paused, savoured the tremor of omnipotence, and blew again. Clouds skittered, swirled, and darkened as the horn blared across the field. He belted out his call over and over again, pacing himself as the pounding in his head grew louder, the blood vessels in his eyes dilated, and the sweat soaked through his shirt. The sense of consummate and utter mastery was unbelievable. No mortal man had ever felt this way.

Boom after boom resounded into the sky, each clamour clustering the clouds as he felt his voice echo through eternity.

Goodspeed blew, breathed, blasted — ignored the pain.

Blasted, breathed, blew.

Twenty, thirty, forty times.

He was in complete control, the clouds obeying his command, coalescing into a cumulonimbus anvil. A giant grey phallus, growing higher with each explosion of breath. Underneath the thunderhead, small tufts of cumulus, in the shape of horse's heads, billowed like outriders. Slowly, the mass swarmed towards him, the horses dragging the looming mountain like some gigantic medieval belfry. Goodspeed's veins wrapped tight around his temples, his eyes bulged from their sockets, and his cheeks flushed crimson.

Still he blew, breathed, blasted.

Fifty, a hundred times.

He lost count.

The wind whipped and whirled around him; the cloud animals dragged the tumult across the river. As the sky lowered, Goodspeed saw riders on the horses, dipping closer and closer as each blast cried out above the noise of the tempest. He could see their spears, shields, and mantles as they descended. Ethereal knights on white warhorses. Goodspeed raised the horn once more, engorged his entire thorax, and sounded an ear-splitting greeting.

Something inside his head exploded.

He was on his back, deaf to the rage of the storm. Despite the excruciating pain, he could see the knights clearly. They were closing on him, their faces masked by helmets, a dark bar atop each white shield. He tried to raise a hand in salute, but he couldn't feel his arm. He tried to smile, but he choked — his throat full of some thick liquid. Goodspeed couldn't hear, couldn't feel, and couldn't breathe, but he could taste the blood and see the horsemen.

As the deluge was unleashed, a pale rider reached down and plucked the Oliphant from his dead fingers.

The Signal Station

Later it developed that he was none other than Lord Northam, of whose ancient hereditary castle on the Yorkshire coast so many odd things were told; but when Williams tried to talk of the castle, and of its reputed Roman origin, he refused to admit that there was anything unusual about it. He even tittered shrilly when the subject of the supposed under crypts, hewn out of the solid crag that frowns on the North Sea, was brought up.

The Descendant, H.P. Lovecraft, 1927

* * *

Angelene did not know anyone when she arrived in Scarborough, and she was still a stranger nine months later, when she departed.

The staff at Springwood Convalescent Home assumed she suffered from an addiction, like their other patients, though they never discovered whether it was drugs, alcohol, men, or work. As spring turned to summer Angelene realised that the cost exceeded the benefits, and moved into a 'licensed private hotel' in Rutland Terrace, on Castle Hill. The next day she paid her first visit to the fortress, set atop the town on the promontory that dominated the coastline. The headland had apparently been occupied for three thousand years, but she was only interested in the last hundred when she bought her ticket at the gift shop in the barbican.

Angelene had chosen the seaside resort for two reasons: it was remote from Canary Wharf, and her grandfather had been stationed there during the First World War. Stanley Cunningham had been a trooper in the Yorkshire Hussars when Scarborough was shelled by two German battleships on the 16th December 1914.

She walked up the steep path to the keep, surprised by the sense of power emanating from the stones. To her left she could see the North Bay, between the castle and the next headland, which jutted out even further into the dark blue sea. To her right the keep loomed, exposed and ruined from an artillery bombardment during the English Civil War. Beyond, the great curtain wall, and below that — out of sight — the town, harbour, and beach hugging the South Bay. As Angelene reached the top of the bluff, a field surrounded by the sea on three sides, a crisp breeze tugged at her long hair.

She ignored the Master Gunner's House and walked around the inner bailey, looking for the remains of the Old Barracks. The German attack had killed nineteen people and destroyed the light-house. Private Cunningham had defended it with a machine gun before being posted to guard what was left of the barracks. He survived the shelling to be gassed and twice wounded on the Western Front. By the time he was demobbed, he'd served in three different regiments in the army and as an ambulance driver in the Royal Flying Corps — all before he was twenty-one. Angelene wished she'd been old enough to remember him, and wished she'd inherited his resilience.

She was disappointed with the barracks, which were no more than a few great stones piled against the curtain wall, all heavily corroded by the wind and sea salt. She continued to the sally port, leading down to the South Steel Battery commanding the lighthouse and harbour. The iron gate was locked as the battery was unstable. She'd hoped for a view of the new lighthouse, but there was nothing to be seen through the bars other than decayed masonry and abundant vegetation. Angelene walked around the diamond-shaped field until she reached what had once been the Roman signal station, identified only by a ditch and the foundations of an enclosure wall and tower. As she walked into the wind, she saw a partially-buried construction which, according to the guide book, was St Mary's Chapel. She shuddered at the thought of an underground place of worship, and made for the fence that marked the eastern boundary of the castle.

The Romans had established a chain of coastal watchtowers to warn of seaborne invasion by the Jutes. Archaeologists believed they were constructed as light-houses, from fifty to a hundred feet high, with at least five floors and a beacon at the top. Around this was a square wall, then a berm, and finally a ditch. Angelene could see the outlines of it all, the stones overgrown by grass as the centuries had passed. She reached the fence and stared down at a sheer drop of well over two hundred feet to Marine Drive. The road had its own defences, great blocks of concrete piled up in the sea to protect it from being reclaimed. As she watched, a wave lapped lazily against the wall — the contact shot it high into the air — the water crashed down onto the promenade, spray whipped by the wind.

Angelene felt unpleasantly exposed to the elements. She decided to go to the exhibition in the Master Gunner's House, but paused at the chapel. It was horrible: a single step descended to a small portcullis, the stones built into the side of a mound like an ancient burial barrow. She wanted to look through the bars into the darkness, but her nerve failed her, and she read the plaque instead. St Mary's Chapel had first been built in 1000, when Scarborough was a Viking settlement, then rebuilt twice after. She hurried away to the Master Gunner's House.

She wandered through the exhibition, finding a reference to the chapel in the section on the Vikings. The town was believed to have been founded by Thorgils Scardi, Thorgils the Hare-Lipped, in 966. There were very few artefacts from this period, the most significant being a book mount and a pair of jet crosses. One of the crosses was in a glass case. Angelene examined it closely. It was a black Maltese cross, with another cross engraved on it. This cross had a semi-circle at each end. Once again, she trembled. She wasn't sure why, but the little black cross with its four sickle shapes was repulsive. The chapel and the cross, there was something offensive about both.

She had a cup of tea and a pastry in the café before braving the fresh air again. The wind blew gently when she emerged and she walked up the steel steps to the keep, marvelling at the bizarre patterns on the eroded stones. It was as if they were calcified or hosted parasites like barnacles or molluscs . . . or something else from the sea. Then she crossed the bailey, passed the well, and walked up another safety staircase to the viewing platform on the curtain wall. She could see several headlands miles away to the south, before the furthest stretched into the sea like a giant pier. To the north, her view was impeded by the very next headland — which was when she had her first epiphany. The geography was wrong: the promontory at Scarborough didn't extend far enough into the sea to make a signal station worthwhile.

She left the castle for the nearest bookshop, where she bought a set of Ordnance Survey maps covering the Roman province of Holderness. She returned to her hotel room, moved her bed, and spread them out on the floor. She had a vague recollection of how to interpret the contour lines and marked the signal stations with a red pen. The total distance from Flamborough to Huntliffe was about fifty miles. Even if the watchtowers were only fifty feet high, the burning beacon would be visible for at least a dozen miles. The coastline could easily have been covered by four stations — five at most — but there were six, all built at the end of the fourth century: Flamborough Head, Filey, Scarborough, Ravenscar, Goldsborough, and Huntcliffe. The most unlikely place for a tower was quite obviously Scarborough, as the fire from Ravenscar to the north would be seen as far south as Filey, if not Flamborough.

Angelene looked out the window to the North Bay and decided that researching the history of the castle was exactly what she needed. She would begin with the German attack in 1914, follow her original plan to discover more about her grandfather, and then work her way back in time until she had solved the mystery of the signal station. It would exercise her mind, and provide a focus where the massages and saunas and holistic therapies had failed.

★　★　★

Angelene quickly established a morning routine which became a meditation. After breakfast she would walk down the meandering path to Royal Albert Drive in North Bay; follow Marine Drive around Castle Hill, past the lighthouse and harbour onto Foreshore Road to the south; then she'd cut up through the Old Town, back to her hotel. On her return, she'd draw a bath, change her clothes, and walk back into town to begin her researches. She started at the library, moved on to the Rotunda Museum a few days later, and then the Creative Industries Centre a few weeks after that.

At the Centre she met Chloe, a freckled brunette with a childlike mouth, sparkling eyes, and a penchant for Celtic jewellery. Chloe instructed her in methodical study and lent her a book called *The Day the East Coast Bled*. Angelene was thrilled to find her grandfather mentioned by name, but her real interest now lay a millennium and a half prior to his small part in the castle's history. As week succeeded week, she ploughed back century by century, ever vigilant for references to the Roman occupation. Weeks became months and she spent less time in the Centre and more scouring the dozen rare and secondhand book dealers in town. She came to know all of them by name, and two in particular benefited from her armchair detection.

At great cost Angelene acquired a modern English translation of Robert Mannyng of Brunne's *Story of Inglande*, completed in 1338. The author claimed to quote from lost Icelandic sagas written about Thorgils and his family founding towns along the Yorkshire coast in the tenth century. There was a reference to a settlement on the headland — as opposed to in the bay — which had been burnt to the ground by Harald Hardrada during his invasion of 1066. It seemed strange that Harald had destroyed whatever was on Castle Hill; commonsense suggested he would have found allies there. A week later Angelene read a scholarly work on the chronicler William of Newburgh, a monk whose writings on Scarborough were dated to the end of the twelfth century. He referred to an Anglo-Saxon monastery on the headland, which

William Le Gros had destroyed before beginning to build the castle in the 1130s. It was the second time the structure on the headland had been purposefully destroyed in less than a century.

There was a gap of nearly six hundred years before the next evidence of a settlement, for which Angelene was grateful. It allowed her to reach the Roman period more quickly without sacrificing the rigour of her studies. One of the first volumes she consulted appeared to solve one mystery, but create another. The author postulated that the purpose of the Scarborough signal station was to alert people inland, rather than on the coast. Angelene was pleased to see he'd used the same geographical evidence she had. She was not, however, convinced. Referring to her maps again, she confirmed that all the Roman settlements inland would've been alerted by the beacon at Filey, which was much better situated.

The new mystery was the archaeological evidence that the watchtower had been occupied for a single year only. Its construction was dated to 383, probably on the orders of Magnus Maximus, the military ruler of Britain. Shortly after, Maximus was proclaimed emperor by his soldiers and left for Gaul. He fought a bloody civil war until his defeat five years later. Fourteen years after his execution, the Romans began their withdrawal from Britain in the face of increasingly bold Anglo-Saxon incursions. The last decade of the fourth century and first decade of the fifth would therefore have been the years when the signal station was most needed.

Angelene read widely on Roman Britain, trying to find as much as she could about the military occupation of Yorkshire. It had begun when the *Legio IX Hispana* crossed the Humber in 71, invading the territory of a Celtic tribe called the Brigantes. She wasn't interested in the headland before the Romans arrived, but she wanted to increase her understanding of their culture. The more she read, however, the further she strayed from her goal. She took to visiting the castle regularly, in order to maintain her focus, but always kept away from the entrance to the chapel. Eventually, she felt her research had stalled entirely. The feeling of well-being which had accompanied her newfound purpose faltered, and she feared the accompanying mental clarity was in danger of being undone. One autumn morning she returned to the Centre and sought out Chloe, and was pleased when she agreed to meet for lunch at a restaurant in the high street.

★   ★   ★

Angelene was nervous. Her self-induced solitude had made her uncomfortable with people. As soon as they'd ordered their food, she blurted out what was on her mind: 'You'll probably think I'm crazy — and maybe I am — but I'm trying to get to the bottom of the Roman signal station, and I thought you might be able to help.'

Chloe's mouth dropped open and she touched her chest reflexively. Or perhaps it was the Celtic torc around her neck. 'I'm not sure what you mean.'

Angelene noticed her tongue dart between her small teeth, pearly white, and felt self-conscious because of the coarseness of her own features. 'I don't think the signal station in Scarborough Castle is part of the coastal chain. I think it was constructed for another reason, but I can't work out why. You seem to have an encyclopaedic knowledge of Scarborough's history . . . ' She trailed off.

Chloe looked relieved. 'I see. Well, there are two theories. First, that the signal station was part of the chain built by Flavius Theodosius in 368, when the Romans restored control of Britain following their losses in the Great Conspiracy. Second, that they were built later, by Magnus Maximus in 383, when he tried to take the Empire for himself. Their purpose would've been to alert the forts inland of an invasion. The Yorkshire Wolds were heavily fortified, because the Brigantes were forever revolting against their Roman overlords.' She touched her torc again.

'Which do you think is right?'

'There's no more historical evidence

for either, but I prefer the latter.'

Angelene leaned forward, lowering her voice as if she was betraying a secret. 'What about the evidence that it was only occupied for a year?'

Chloe cleared her throat delicately. 'That's one of the points in favour of Maximus constructing it. As soon as his armies proclaimed him emperor he left for Gaul to fight for control of the Empire. One of the beautiful things about ancient history is that it's more art than science, and open to different interpretations.'

'But what about the Viking attack in 1066? Why did they burn everything on the headland? And what about William of Newburgh? He wrote that William Le Gros destroyed an Anglo-Saxon monastery on the headland before he started building the castle seventy years later! I think . . . I'm not sure what to think . . . ' She felt her confidence disappear.

Chloe reached over and placed her dainty hand on Angelene's forearm. Her touch was light and cool. 'I've got something you might be interested in reading. Come back to the Centre with me after lunch and I'll give you a copy. Read it, then you can tell me what you think.'

Angelene tried to smile. 'What is it?'

'My doctoral thesis. It has a dreadfully long title, but it's basically about Caesar's invasion of Britain, viewed from the Britons' perspective, and it draws on Geoffrey of Monmouth's Historia Regnum Brittania, *The Matter of Britain*, and Nennius's Historia Brittonum. It deals with the period four hundred years before the signal station was built, but you may find it . . . relevant. No more questions until you've read it, yes?'

Angelene agreed, wondering what the signal station could possibly have to do with Caesar's invasion when the Romans hadn't reached Yorkshire until long after the famous emperor's death.

★   ★   ★

She was still wondering in the early hours of the next morning when she was about a third of the way through the five hundred page manuscript. A large part of the thesis was about the druids, their slaughter at Anglesey, and the belief that the Romans had called upon malign powers to defeat the magic of the British. There were theories concerning the importance of Stonehenge, Glastonbury, Cerne Abbas, Wilmington, Uffington, and various other ancient places she'd heard of. When she could no longer keep her eyes open, she dropped the manuscript on the floor next to her — probably waking the whole household — and closed her eyes.

Angelene forced herself to rise when the alarm went off a few hours later, had breakfast, and took her morning exercise. After her bath, she removed Chloe's dissertation downstairs to the residents' lounge, and picked up where she'd left off. There was more about druids and bards, and their beliefs, traditions, and practices. These included the significance of torcs, skulls, standing stones, and the ogham script, as well as notes on the gods they worshipped, including Belenus, patron of the druids, and the goddess Brigantia, from whom she assumed the Brigantes tribe had taken their name. There was only a brief mention of the acknowledged gods of the Romans, with more detail about the sea demons they were supposed to have summoned.

Chloe had used 'sea demons' as a descriptive term for these creatures, called the Cth by the Romans, Fomorians by the Parisii, and Old Ones by the Brigantes. They were a powerful, ancient race of immortals that lived under the waves and were summoned by human sacrifice. They were said to feed on the fear of humans and steal the souls of the dead and living alike. The presence of the sea demons explained why the druidic stronghold in Anglesey had been defeated so easily: it was an island, completely surrounded by the water from which the creatures came. With the help of the Cth, the Romans had taken the island and completely obliterated the druidic religion. Angelene wondered if Chloe had actually been awarded her PhD. She never used the title 'doctor' and Angelene couldn't recall seeing it mentioned at the Centre. Her thesis had probably been rejected.

Nonetheless Angelene applied herself

to it all through the day and long into the evening, breaking only for supper. She finished around midnight, her eyes aching and her mind racing, full of Chloe's wild ideas and fanciful speculations. As she prepared for bed, Angelene made a conscious effort to try and understand why Chloe felt the thesis was relevant to the signal station. She agreed with Chloe that it had been built by Maximus in 383, but what purpose had it served him? Angelene didn't believe the beacon was meant to communicate with the Wolds to the west. It didn't feel right. Nor was it meant to be seen by the other coastal stations to the north and south. If not west, north, or south . . .

Angelene had her second epiphany the moment she switched off the light.

Maximus had been preparing to usurp the emperor and steal the crown of the mightiest empire the world had ever known. He'd believed in the sea demons. He'd built the station as a temple to them and tried to summon their assistance in his bid for the Empire. That was it. It explained everything. It had only been occupied for a short time because Maximus had left Britain soon after. She knew she was right and planned to find out more about Maximus' final years in Gaul. She was filled with optimism that her peace of mind had finally been restored, and slept more soundly than she had in years.

★ ★ ★

At six o'clock the next evening, Angelene knocked on a mahogany door decorated with a carving of the Green Man.

Chloe opened it a few moments later. 'Oh, hello, I wasn't expecting you. But come in, please.'

Angelene stepped into a sylvan sanctuary. The cottage was small and cosy, a sacred space with hardwood floors and timber in the walls and ceiling. There was wood of all types and colours almost everywhere in furniture, ornaments, and frames. Leafy pot plants commanded the hall, the lounge, and the kitchen beyond, and there was a sprig of mistletoe above the door. She felt as if she were inside a magic womb. 'I read your thesis. I thought I'd return it in person. I hope you don't mind?'

Chloe led her into the lounge. 'No, of course not. Make yourself comfortable.' She indicated a settee. 'Would you like a cup of tea?'

'Yes, please.'

While she waited, Angelene walked around the room. Between the plants and Celtic symbols on the walls there were landscape photos of various places in Britain. Stone circles, groves, forests, and chalk figures. 'Did you take these yourself?' she asked when Chloe returned.

'Some of them. There you are.' She handed Angelene a cup and saucer, placed a teapot on a low oak table, and sat in a wicker chair. 'I suppose you didn't find my thesis very useful. I'm sorry if it's been a waste of time.'

'Not at all. I'll admit that half the time I was reading I wondered why on earth you'd given it to me, but when I reached the end, I realised.'

'You finished it!' Chloe's surprise, like all her other expressions, was refined.

'Yes. It was only when I finished that the answer came to me. I know everything!'

Chloe upset her teacup, spilling some on her blouse. Angelene could've sworn she'd touched the torc again. 'How stupid of me.' Chloe glided into the kitchen and returned with a tea towel, dabbing the chair and her top. She left her cup and saucer on the table when she sat down again. 'What do you know?' There was a hard edge to her voice Angelene hadn't heard before.

'About the signal station!' She hesitated, suddenly wondering if she'd finally gone mad. But she couldn't be mad, she felt too calm and satisfied. 'I'm convinced that Magnus Maximus had the signal station built because he was another believer in the sea demons you mentioned. He built it as a kind of temple to summon their aid. He believed that they'd helped Caesar conquer Britannia, and he wanted their help in his conquest of the Empire. He built it to summon them, then — when it didn't work — he abandoned it and took his men to Gaul to fight. It explains all the discrepancies. I'm right, aren't I?'

Chloe sighed, and laughed nervously. 'Yes, that's exactly what I think. Well done you!' She smiled, revealing her tiny teeth again.

'I went up to the castle this morning after my walk, and spent an hour at the signal station. I wasn't sure my idea would make any sense in the cold light of day, but when I stood there, looking out to sea and thinking about those sea demons, I knew I was right. Poor old Maximus, he should've put his time to better use!'

'You're quite right. It didn't help him at all.'

'I came here to convalesce and . . . I feel wonderful. It's taken me long enough, but immersing myself in something so distant from my life has been the most therapeutic thing ever. I'm ready to go back to London now. I'm leaving on Friday. I can't thank you enough for all your help, Chloe, you've been wonderful.'

Chloe's tension evaporated in an instant. 'I'm sorry you're leaving, but I'm glad you found the peace you were looking for. I hope you don't mind, but I've bought you something. Perhaps you'll wear it as a memento of your time here.' Chloe picked up a small cardboard box from the sideboard, and withdrew a thick bronze bangle. It was in the shape of a torc, exactly like the one around her neck, but smaller. 'Here . . . '

Angelene took it from her and studied the plain circle of metal. 'Thank you, it's lovely. Are you sure you want me to have it?'

'Yes, of course. Perhaps you'll try it on now.'

Angelene slipped it onto her right wrist. 'Oh, a perfect fit. Thank you.'

Later that night Angelene walked out the bathroom and raised her hand to switch off the light. She saw the bracelet and stopped her arm in mid-air. She touched the cool metal with her fingertips and was about to slide it off when she had her third epiphany. It was more consummate than the others. It was also calamitous and frightening, and she left both light and torc alone as she sat on the bed. She *must* be going mad, but she still felt poised and collected. Some time passed before she switched the light off and went to her window. She looked out at the dark, deep sea and knew she had to find out for herself.

★ ★ ★

The castle closed at five o'clock. Angelene watched the visitors shuffle off to the entrance as a member of staff did his rounds. Then the women in the Master Gunner's House locked up and left. As the young man closing the castle climbed the steps to the keep, she withdrew into one of the stone alcoves, concealing herself in a corner. She heard his footsteps on the wooden platform before he trotted back down the steel stairway. She waited for another hour before she risked leaving her hiding place. She'd never done anything like this before, so she could only hope she'd prepared adequately. Her hair was tied back in a tight ponytail, Chloe's gift was snug on her wrist, and she wore her walking boots.

In her backpack, she carried a flask of tea, a powerful flashlight, and a small bolt-cutter.

The wind howled and the clouds moved briskly across the sickle moon as the sun began to set. Angelene could see the mound of St Mary's chapel clearly despite the failing light. It was uncanny, because sixteen hundred years ago there'd been a huge tower here, perhaps as tall as the keep behind her, and no chapel. Now, there was only the chapel, the foundation stones from the station all but invisible. She stopped a few feet from the mound, removed the flashlight from her pack, and switched it on.

The beam illuminated the small portcullis gate and beige stone in the blackness beyond. Angelene held the torch in her left hand and the backpack in her right. She took a deep breath and a single step. She swallowed, dropped the backpack on the grass, and glanced at the sliding bolt.

She almost screamed: the padlock was gone.

It had been there ten hours ago; she'd seen it with her own eyes. She reached out her hand and gave the iron a gentle push.

It shrieked as it swung back an inch.

Angelene's heart beat a frenzied tattoo. She felt a lump in her throat. She tried to swallow, failed, and was nearly sick. She gasped for breath.

She could see into the subterranean chapel. It was small, a rough square with each stone wall about twenty feet in length and seven in height. There was a square enclosure in the centre, with low walls four feet long. She couldn't see what was inside, but thought it might be another well.

She fought to bring her breathing under control, then pushed the gate open, and ducked in.

She trod slowly and carefully down the two steps to the uneven floor.

Angelene was in a tomb — or a temple — anything but a chapel.

She held the light ahead of her protectively and advanced towards the centre square. She was scared, but it seemed to draw her with an ominous inevitability. As she approached she could see a shadow within the four walls. She turned the beam —

'Angelene.'

She slapped her right hand over her mouth to stop herself screaming and spun towards the voice.

Chloe stood in the corner, one hand clutching the torc around her throat.

Angelene grunted, choked — only when she was sure she wouldn't scream did she take her hand away from her mouth.

'I was afraid you'd come,' said Chloe.

'You — you — scared me to death. What the hell are you doing here?' Her fear was replaced by sudden, vicious anger.

'I'm here to stop you . . . ' Chloe pointed past Angelene to the middle of the vault ' . . . seeing.'

Angelene turned her light on the enclosure and moved forward.

'It's a stairway to the prison — where the Romans kept the human sacrifices before they killed them. You know the secret now, so let's leave together.'

Angelene shone the torch over the wall

and saw narrow stone stairs winding down, curling in a tight circle. 'I'm not going anywhere with you. You tried to scare me last night with this bangle and now you've done it again. I'm going to have a look at this dungeon, satisfy myself that I'm right, and then get back to my life. I've had enough of you and your crackpot thesis. You're as bad as those murderous, power-crazed, Romans.' She swung her leg over the wall.

'No!'

'Don't try to stop me!' She shone the light at Chloe, but she hadn't moved.

'If you won't heed my warning, take this.' Chloe shook the torc, which she was still clutching. 'Your circlet isn't enough — *please* take my torc as well.'

Angelene waved her right wrist. 'I don't even know why I'm still wearing this ugly thing.'

'Please — Angelene — if you value your sanity, please wear my torc.'

Angelene scowled, swung her other leg over the wall, and began her descent. Chloe started chanting in a language that sounded like German. Angelene swore.

She wasn't scared by this absurd hocus-pocus, and she ignored the mantra and concentrated on her feet. The smooth stone steps were steep, and they spiralled to the left. It was just like any other medieval staircase and there was nothing unusual or unsettling about the journey. Angelene estimated that she descended roughly a foot with each step, and that Marine Drive was about two hundred and fifty feet below at the most. She probably wouldn't even get close to sea level, but she counted as she went anyway.

After a hundred and fifty steps the staircase widened, the steps ceased to spiral as tightly, and the limestone lining was replaced by the natural, blue-tinted Oxford Clay. She had the impression she was approaching another vault or a chamber, but there was nothing of the sort. The air grew stale and the rock damp. Angelene felt the sweat of the walls as she brushed against them.

At two hundred and fifty feet she reached the flaxen bedrock, and the stairs took a more meandering course, no longer winding, but still descending. She could hear the crash of the waves, echoing from all directions in the enclosed space of the tunnel. The smell of salt was strong, mixed with a whiff of mildew, and something stronger that reminded her of decaying flesh. Water dripped down the walls and Angelene had to slow her pace as the steps became slippery. She could no longer gauge the rate of her descent but continued to count each footfall.

By three hundred steps the smell was like a charnel house. The walls were heavily pitted, similar to the stone of the castle above, and there was a steady trickle of water flowing down the stairs.

As she counted her four hundredth step, Angelene saw the end of the stairway far below, terminating at the entrance to a cave. She was tempted to speed up, but remembered the water underfoot. The last few stairs were completely submerged.

At four hundred and eighty four paces, she reached the bottom, standing in seawater midway up her shins. The rotten smell was even stronger, as if there were a carcass of something large nearby.

She waded cautiously forward, shining the light into the narrow tunnel ahead. Angelene was wary of the water level, but it appeared unchanged, and she could feel a gentle current pulling ahead. The adit was wide and high enough for her to pass easily, and the water didn't creep any further up her legs. She walked a few more paces as the tunnel curved, and then saw it open into a vault. She pushed forward with renewed energy, ignoring the rising water, and paused at the entrance to an immense cavern which extended beyond the illumination of her torch. The water reached her knees and the stench would have been unbearable were it not for the sharp tang of salt. She couldn't see an end to either the sandstone walls or the still, dark water and knew she couldn't go much further. She was disappointed to find the prison flooded.

Angelene heard a soft splash — felt a slight eddy in the water.

She peered ahead, but still couldn't see anything.

She heard another splash, fainter and further away.

She waded forward — saw something in the mere about fifty feet ahead. She pressed on until the water was midway up her thighs. Then she stopped, held the flashlight at arm's length, and strained to discern the details of the pale grey mound now thirty feet away. It appeared to be a lump of clay about twenty feet across and ten or so high, curiously crisscrossed with thick, black lines that reminded her of a small railway track. The front of the mound was shaped like a polyp, behind which was a single, luminous ellipse, yellowy in colour.

Angelene saw the lines were in fact links in a massive metal chain, rusted with age. She wondered why they'd been left on an island in the middle of the lake.

The chains creaked as the clay twitched.

The ellipse disappeared and reappeared. It blinked.

She stared at that eye in the huge, formless creature, and screamed and screamed and screamed.

★ ★ ★

The next morning Angelene left the hotel for her morning ritual. She was mentally and physically exhausted, but she weaved her way down to Royal Albert Drive, too afraid to look at the headland. Only when she reached the road, did she realise she was on the very edge of the sea. She didn't know which was worse, what lay beneath the castle or what lay beneath the ocean. She shivered and hesitated.

She remembered Chloe's words from a few hours before. The thing was a prisoner, because neither the Pagans nor the Christians had the power to kill it. It was alive, but it couldn't escape.

Angelene continued until the promenade began to curve around Castle Hill. She stopped again, and reached for her right wrist. Why had she taken off the bangle when she'd dressed? It — and Chloe's chanting — had prevented her from losing her mind. She faltered. She lacked the courage to walk in between that . . . thing . . . and the dark, swirling sea. Angelene turned to go back, then caught a glimpse of a teenager on a bicycle. He was pedalling towards her, crossing the very path she feared to tread. She was being stupid, paranoid.

She took a deep breath, smiled at the boy as he passed, and resumed her circuit.

The cyclist was the only witness to the freak wave that crashed against the sea wall, picked Angelene up from Marine Drive, and lifted her over the cast-iron railings and the blocks of quartz. He was the first of hundreds to look for her body, but it was never found.

Devil's Own

Todd turned off the dirt track and saw the old man waiting for him in the farmyard. Todd waved, parked his land rover next to a tractor, and joined him.

'You must be the man from Natural England,' the farmer said. He was smoking a foul-smelling pipe with one hand and kept the other firmly in his pocket.

'Yes, my name's Todd; pleased to meet you.'

'I'm Griffiths, New Mill Farm is mine.' Todd wasn't sure if a response was expected, so he just nodded. An awkward silence descended. 'You'll be wanting to see the trees, then?'

'That's why I'm here.' Todd smiled.

Griffiths inclined his head to the right. 'They're up there. Castle Hill Wood.' Todd could see a copse on a low hill about a quarter of a mile away. 'It's the beeches, not the pines. There's a dozen of them.'

Todd waited for more information, but

none was forthcoming. 'Thank you, Mr Griffiths, I'll go and have a look. I'll let you know when I'm done.' He walked back to his vehicle.

'You won't get far in that. Have to use your legs, get some exercise.'

'All right.' Todd took his camera from the land rover.

'If it is a new species, will they let me name it?'

'I doubt it,' said Todd, hoping to needle him.

Griffiths scowled.

Todd whistled as he strolled down to the track. Presently, he heard the sound of running water, and reached a path that followed the curve of the beck to the foot of the hill. He identified the beeches in the centre of the wood long before he entered the trees; they rose to about eighty feet, double the size of the surrounding pines. Due to the leafy canopy above, the undergrowth was sparse and he negotiated the slope with ease.

Todd stopped to take his bearings after a couple of minutes, running his fingers along the rough scales of the nearest bole. The bark was dark grey and scaly, typical of the Scots Pine, one of the most common species of the genus. He estimated the grove was about six hundred square feet in size, a rough triangle with its apex at Cock Beck and base at the crest of Castle Hill. It was cool in the shade, and he savoured the smells of the forest, a mixture of leaf and wood tinged with a slight taint of decay. He could hear the stream clearly, but was surprised at the absence of bird calls.

Todd kept his eyes peeled for the silver bark of the beech trees as he resumed his ascent, but found the first by its roots rather than colour. He was halfway up the hill when he noticed the thick, twisted limbs hooked into the earth like talons. The roots and the lower part of the tree trunk were green, completely covered in lichen. He moved to a second, larger tree and touched the bare bark, which was smooth and damp. They were clearly European Beeches, also very common, and he wondered why Griffiths had reported the discovery of a new species.

Todd took a step back, careful not to trip on the labyrinthine root system. The bark was in fact a little dark for a beech tree — ranging from chestnut whcre the lichen ended to the more usual silver a few feet up — but not remarkably so. He took another couple of tentative steps back and switched on his camera. While he was waiting for it to load, his attention was caught by a row of tiny beige pebbles between two buttress roots. They looked like minute bits of bone and he knelt down and tried to pick one up.

Todd gasped for breath — jumped up — stumbled.

He was staring at the exposed mouth of a grinning human skull.

★　★　★

'Of course there's a skeleton in the woods,' said Griffiths, still gnawing on his pipe. 'What about my beeches?'

'No, I'm serious. I can't get any reception on my mobile. May I use your phone?'

'I know you're serious.' Griffiths didn't

move from the doorway.

'It's a crime scene; I have to let the police know immediately.'

Griffiths guffawed, removed his pipe, and bared his stained teeth. 'Don't you know where you are, sonny?'

'Yes, of course. I'm two and a half miles south of Tadcaster, near a village called Saxton, and that's what I'm going to tell the police. If you won't — '

'You're on Towton battlefield. Five hundred and fifty years ago thirty thousand men were killed here.'

'Thirty thousand?' Todd repeated in disbelief.

'Aye, the Wars of the Roses. I'll show you.' Griffiths pushed past Todd into the yard and pointed east, to the main road. 'They lined up there, on t'other side. The Yorkists opposite us, the Lancastrians further north, near Towton village. Palm Sunday, 1461, in the middle of a snowstorm.' Griffiths turned to face the wood. 'They were evenly matched, but the Lancastrians had the high ground. Their problem was the wind. It blew the snow in their faces and took the edge off their arrows. They got fed up of getting shot by the Yorkist archers, came down to engage, and were butchered. Hence Bloody Meadow, over there.' He waved to the north.

'Surely thirty thousand dead is an exaggeration?'

'Most of the Lancastrians were killed trying to cross the river, but King Edward and the Duke of Somerset both agreed on no quarter before the battle. The wounded were slaughtered like lambs. They're buried in mass graves all over the place. Ten years ago some clever knobs from Bradford University dug up forty-three skeletons. I don't think there's been any bodies found on Castle Hill yet, but there's a legend that Black MacSween and his Jock mercenaries made their last stand there.'

Griffiths spat into the ground at Todd's feet.

'So-called because of his raven black hair and evil ways; supposed to have made a bargain with the devil to do his work in return for eternal life. Nowt good it did him. He and his men died up there with all the rest. Maybe you found old Black Mac, but I want to know about them trees. Do you see what I mean about the bark?'

* * *

Todd felt the weight of history on his shoulders when he returned to Castle Hill armed with a camera, a spade, and a pair of secateurs. Even though he was expecting it, the sight of the skull unnerved him, a hideous reminder of the thousands of dead underfoot. He counted twelve beech trees in total, eleven of them arranged around the largest, which was about a hundred feet high and seven in diameter. He approached the great tree, but still couldn't see anything remarkable about it except for the slight discolouration of the bark above the lichen line.

Todd was reluctant to make a fool of himself for a second time, however, so he put the tools down and drew his lock knife. He rested his knee against one of the buttress roots and ran his fingers up and down the lichen. The fungus was a sign of a healthy tree and he had never seen it so thick or so abundant. Though it was against all his instincts, he scraped at the top of the moist green crust, exposing a patch of chestnut bark. Then he selected a spot lower down the trunk, and scraped again. The change in colour was pronounced. Instead of a shade of brown, it was a dark, burnt red. With mounting excitement, he moved his knife over the top of one of the roots. He grabbed the fleshy tuber with his free hand and rubbed the blade back and forth with renewed vigour.

Crimson.

The root was a rich crimson under its green coat. Todd selected another tree and repeated his performance, with the same result. He tried a third, just to make sure, but needn't have bothered. It seemed the obnoxious old man was right and Castle Hill had indeed spawned a new species of beech. Todd returned to the great tree and made the three bare patches larger. He put away his knife, switched on his camera, and took half a dozen photos. When he was finished, he decided to take a sample cutting from a root as the branches were out of reach.

While the massive tendrils appeared deeply embedded in the earth, the system was actually very shallow, and the illusory stability made Todd think of the claws of an arthritic giant, too gnarled and diseased to grip with any potency. He shuddered at the thought, picked up his spade, and exposed the lower part of one of the secondary roots. Due to the absence of lichen, it was bright crimson, repellent to the eye. He brushed away the loose soil, and snapped another photo. Then he took the secateurs and positioned them fifteen centimetres from the end.

Todd paused, feeling as if he was about to cut a living vein. Of course he was. Trees were alive and their roots were their veins, arteries sucking the strength from the land. He attempted to laugh it off, failed, clasped the secateurs — stopped. He couldn't help imagining the massive, misshapen talon feeding off the litres and litres of blood soaked into the soil.

Todd forced the picture from his mind,

gripped the secateurs tight, and squeezed the handles together.

There was a squelching sound followed by a loud snap as a spray of blood spurted into the air.

He cried out — fell back — scrabbled to his feet.

The root was bleeding.

He turned to run, tripped, and lost consciousness when his head hit the ground.

⋆　⋆　⋆

Todd opened his eyes, saw leaves and branches high above, the blue sky beyond. His head and right leg hurt; he could hear running water. He realised where he was, remembered what had happened, and raised his head. Pain sliced through his skull so he turned it to the right instead, which wasn't as bad. He was lying at the foot of the great beech, his legs on the roots, his head and torso slightly lower down the slope. He knew he should try and change position to stop the blood from flowing to his head, so he started to roll over towards the tree. This time the pain came from his ankle, and he was unable to complete the manoeuvre. Eventually, by bending at the waist and pushing with his elbows, he identified the new source of discomfort.

At first Todd thought he was hallucinating. Somehow he'd managed to wedge his right foot underneath the arch of a lichen-covered root. He couldn't work out how it had happened, but the evidence was irrefutable. He used his elbows to push himself away, but had to stop because of the pain. His foot was stuck fast, his ankle probably broken. Perhaps the break accounted for his entanglement, yet there were few places where the roots didn't actually touch the ground. Maybe his foot had dug under the root as he fell. Whatever the cause, it was an incredible stroke of bad luck. He couldn't see the bloody stump of the root he'd cut, but the blood was there, literally on his hands.

Todd lay still for a while, trying to keep calm. A breeze stirred the leaves above and he resolved to call for help. He began with a few timid cries, wary of his sore head. When he found it didn't hurt, he opened his lungs and bellowed for all he was worth. He shouted, paused for a few seconds, and shouted again. There was no answer, just the sound of the water below and the wind above. He called over and over again, panic rising with each effort.

Some time before he grew hoarse, he passed out.

★ ★ ★

Todd woke to the sensation of something creeping up his leg. The forest was darker and the wind louder. He felt pressure on his shin, looked down, screamed. A thick green tentacle was wrapped three times around his lower leg, all the way up to the knee. He kicked with his left leg and flailed with his arms, ignoring the pain coursing through his body. He grunted through gritted teeth as he tried to drag himself free, but the grip of the great beech was too strong.

The only results of Todd's supreme effort were specks of white light flashing in his eyes and an urge to vomit.

He lay back, blinking, sweating, and gasping for breath. Behind him, the nearest beech tree was less than ten feet away. It had been more than double that distance before he'd fallen. He looked to his right, then left, then craned his neck. They were all closer. All the beeches had crept closer to him, crawling on their blind, arboreal feelers.

Todd tried to scream, but his throat was too raw.

He coughed and choked, remembered his knife. He removed it from his pocket, fumbled with sweat-slicked hands, and freed the blade. The root was even tighter now, and further up his leg. He twisted his aching body, reversed the knife, and hacked at the coiled green snake. Only the tip of the blade penetrated the ancient wood. He hacked again, missed, and drove the knife into his shin.

He lost consciousness when the metal touched bone.

★ ★ ★

Todd saw the light of the moon and heard the rustle of leaves over the whistle of wind. He could feel the root in his thigh. Not around, but *inside*. He attempted to lift his head, failed. Eleven roots from eleven trees pinned every part of his body to the ground. A gust of wind buffeted the boughs and the great beech bent low. Todd could have sworn that the topmost leaves were pitch black, like the feathers of a raven.

Spurn

I was thinking about drowning when the child stepped out from behind the 'enforcement cameras' sign.

I slammed on the brakes.

Even though I was only crawling along, the car sluiced across the motorway-turned-river, straight for him.

I closed my eyes at the last instant, but when the impact came it was from behind, not in front. As I'd expected — or hoped.

I should be used to this shit by now.

I pulled over to the hard shoulder, tried to calm my nerves, and stepped out into the unrelenting rain. The good news was that the car was a monster SUV, so I hadn't done any damage with my little MX5. The bad news was that the driver was almost as big as his car, a skinhead with a boxer's nose and rugby player's ears. I thought he was going to rip my head off, but I'm at the stage where I really couldn't care less, so I joined him in the space between our vehicles.

I was right: no damage to his, a big dent in my rear end. I told him a dog had run out across the motorway, and he bought it. We exchanged details in the downpour and he asked me if my car would be all right to drive. I said yes to get rid of him. I returned to the convertible, watched him pull back out into the traffic, and chucked his details out the window.

Obviously, I'm not going to claim this one on the insurance either.

I waited for the Big Friendly Giant to disappear into the cataract, and resumed my journey east. It's Friday the twenty-ninth of October, East Yorkshire is saturated, and one of my editors has sent me to cover Halloween at Dane's Dyke. Dane's Dyke is a forest near Flamborough Head, which forms the northern part of Bridlington Bay. It's become a big occult centre since a BBC news piece unwittingly featured evidence of a haunting during a broadcast in the late eighties. I don't believe in ghosts, but

I do believe in money, and money always follows a good story. Word is that this year the Satanists are going to provide one by descending on Dane's Dyke en masse and doing — whatever Satanists do. I think it's a recognised religion these days, so I'm not expecting human sacrifice; but whatever they get up to, I'll be there to watch.

Howden was a diversion courtesy of the booklet lying on my passenger seat: *13 Horror Stories from Holderness*. It was the last thing Gwen gave me. She must have bought it a while ago, because even though we haven't spoken in five months, it arrived in the post on my birthday. I wasn't surprised. Gwen can be unspeakably kind and delightfully cruel — and often at the same time. All thirteen tales are traditional ghost stories set in what was once known as Holderness, the Yorkshire coast from Flamborough Head to Spurn Point. In Roman times, Holderness extended three miles east of today's shore, but the coastline has been submerged over the years as the sea gradually eroded and inundated the soft rock. The idea of the thirty-odd settlements now lying so close under the water disturbs me, but I think there might be a story in the city of Lod, which was not only the biggest of the drowned towns, but also had the most dramatic end.

I found the right junction and followed the signs to the small market town. Once upon a time Howden must have been a lot more important than it is now, because it still sports a great big thirteenth century gothic cathedral in the style of York and Beverley Minsters. I should have gone straight to Flamborough to start nosing about for some back-story on the Satanists, but I'd decided on two stops en route. The *Evening Post* might be paying for Dane's Dyke, but when you're freelance, you've got to try and make the most of your research. I can give the *Post* their story and do a piece on Lod for something a little more highbrow, maybe the *Express* or *Mail*.

I parked in the centre of the town, the spires of the minster looming ominously above. The rain had eased to a drizzle, so

I took my little Nikon along, stuffing it in one pocket and *13 Horror Stories* in another.

I turned the corner to enter the grounds of the Parish Church of St Peter and St Paul, and stopped dead: the huge chancel was in ruins.

This couldn't be right. I'd Googled Howden Minster yesterday; it was a fully-functioning church. I had a sudden fear that I'd lost the ability to tell what was real and what was imagined. I suppose it wasn't really sudden, because it's something I've been thinking about more and more of late. I'm not going to get into that now . . .

I walked further into the churchyard. The colour of the stone changed from beige to bone and I remembered the minster was constructed with limestone. To my relief, I discovered that the nave was intact, but the dark, decorative arches supporting nothing and leading nowhere were eerie, like the shadow of a cathedral. A distant, decaying memory of better days.

As there were still a few minutes left

before the communion service finished, I decided to see if I couldn't find what I was after by myself. According to *13 Horror Stories*, the only remaining evidence of Lod is the market cross, which was saved and removed to the churchyard of Howden. The graveyard ran along the southern side of the minster, with the headstones ordered in neat lines amidst overgrown vegetation. I wandered down the aisles searching for anything dating back to the fourteenth century, though I wasn't sure how much of the cross would be left after six hundred years or more of exposure to the elements. I squelched through the puddles and mud, but couldn't find anything more than two hundred years old.

Presently I saw a few people leave the minster by a pair of wooden doors under a trio of vertical stained glass windows. I smiled at a couple of elderly parishioners, and entered the transept. A large clergyman looking like a blonde Brian Blessed was talking to three old ladies. To my right, a recess housed a chapel commemorating the war dead. On my left, various pamphlets, leaflets, and booklets were arranged on a table. I flicked through *Howden Minster, A Guide Book*, and was just finishing a paragraph on the collapse of the chancel roof in 1758 when I was disturbed by a grating cough.

Brian Blessed and I were alone.

'Hello, Mr Slaughter, I'm Grant Markham.' The Reverend Cedric Slaughter chose to regard me with disdain instead of taking my extended hand. He was almost as big as the skinhead, and a lot fiercer. I dropped my hand and continued. 'I'm a journalist doing a story on the lost towns of Holderness. I read that the market cross from Lod is in your churchyard?' When he failed to reply, I tried the direct approach: 'Is it here?'

His eyes darted to a grey stone pillar lying on the floor next to the chapel. 'I think you need to go back and do your research properly, Mr Markham. Nothing remains of Lod, or Ravenser Odd, but there's a cross commemorating the arrival of King Henry IV in Ravenser in 1399. Ravenser also lies under the water now, and the cross is in Kilnsea.' He moved closer, ushering me towards the door.

I held my ground. 'What's that?' I pointed at the pillar on the flagstones.

He was very close, one great arm encircling — but not quite touching — me. 'If you would like a guided tour of the minster, I suggest you make an appointment with the sexton.' He moved further forward, so his face was only inches from mine.

I stepped to the side, away from him and the door. 'I don't want a guided tour, Mr Slaughter. I want to know what that stone is.'

His cold blue eyes held mine for a few seconds, and then he obviously decided it would be easier to humour me. 'It's from the original Norman church.'

'So it dates back to the thirteenth century?'

'Before that — long before that. The minster is closed, Mr Markham, I'd like you to leave.' He raised his arm again, indicating the doorway.

As I walked out into the rain, the door slammed shut behind me. I was retracing my steps past the ruined chancel when my mobile rang. I stopped in the

132

graveyard. 'Hello?'

Silence.

'Hello!'

'Grant . . . ' A woman's voice; it sounded as if she was crying.

'Gwen? Gwen, is that you? It's me. Talk to me!'

Whoever it was put the phone down.

I checked the last incoming call and saw 'number withheld'. Could it have been her? She hadn't spoken to me since she left, but she did send me the booklet, so I knew I wasn't forgotten. I put the phone back in my pocket, and walked out into Market Place.

The deluge had resumed and it seemed as if the whole of East Yorkshire was drowning. No wonder all these Ravensers disappeared. *13 Horror Stories* was written by Rethuel Scarcig — one of those randomly generated pen names if ever I've seen one — and published by The Preceptory Players, of 5–7 Vicar Lane, Howden. I found the narrow, Georgian alley easily, then the right house number, belonging to the Howden Bookshop. The premises had both sets of windows boarded up — which was strange, because I'd phoned to check their hours of business only two days ago.

★ ★ ★

Saturday the thirtieth of October. I'm sitting on a rock at the foot of a dune on the eastern shore of the Spurn Peninsula as I dictate this, looking out to Lod in what I'm sure will be a short interruption of service in the downpour.

I spent the rest of yesterday driving through the rivers of Babylon — AKA the roads around Hull — to Kilnsea. New Kilnsea actually, as Old Kilnsea is under the sea like the rest of the county will be if this rain continues. Everything took longer than it should have, and on top of it all, there's no cross there either. I asked some local halfwit and he told me he'd never heard of Ravenser — Odd, or any other — or Lod. Waste of time. I stayed in a shitty B&B in another little dump called Easington, and overslept.

At midday, stuck on the narrow road between Easington and Kilnsea, I realised the folly of this Gwen-inspired diversion. Up ahead there were temporary traffic lights, and the northbound lane was blocked. It was raining harder than ever and the road was completely flooded. As I inched closer I saw a mains pipe had burst and water was gushing out from the roadside while workmen waded around in wellies. The drainage ditches on the side of the road were full, and pools of water covered the fields.

I had the feeling that if I continued making for Spurn, I'd be cut off from the rest of England, and either slide into the sea, or disappear under floodwaters.

The light ahead turned green and I drove carefully through the overflow. At Kilnsea I took Spurn Road and drove to the entrance of Spurn Point Nature Reserve. I left my car at the warden's lodge and set off on foot. The reserve covers the last three miles of coastline, a skinny peninsula called Spurn Head. The strip of land curves back west like the tail of a 'y' and the very end is known as Spurn Point. Instead of walking to Spurn Point, I headed for the beach on the eastern side, armed with an Ordnance Survey map, a printed download, and a compass.

Lod existed between 1200 and 1360, growing until it rivalled Kingston-upon-Hull by the beginning of the fourteenth century. Rivalling what is now considered England's worst city doesn't sound very impressive, but Hull was the country's second biggest port until about 1600. First syphilis and then the *Luftwaffe* made it what it is today. Unlike the other towns and villages along the Yorkshire coast, the inundation of Lod happened quickly, while people were still living there. The last days were also faithfully recorded by the monks, and Abbot Burton of Meaux wrote: 'by its wicked works and piracies, it provoked the wrath of God against itself beyond measure.' Although the town had been losing ground to the water for several years, the abbot described scenes of panic and flight as the last part of the city was claimed by the sea in a flood of biblical proportions circa 1360.

A strong north-easterly wind was blowing the rain into my face, but it had at least eased off to a drizzle again. I marched onto the wet sand and stared at the great mass of water beyond. The North Sea: cold, treacherous, inhospitable; fatal to seafarers and landsmen alike. I read that storm surges have claimed over two hundred thousand lives since records began in the twelfth century. If you're Dutch or German you don't even have to go swimming to drown — the sea comes to you.

Up the coast, I could see a rocky outcrop. I fished out the compass and the OS map, and worked out it must be the remainder of the Second World War coastal defences — also partly submerged. I couldn't see very far south, because of the curve of the spit. The exact location of Lod is a mile and a half south-east of Spurn Point. Or rather, where Spurn Point was in the fourteenth century. While the coastline is retreating steadily westward, Spurn Point erodes and rebuilds itself every two hundred and fifty years. Something about longshore drift, apparently. I scrutinised the second map, which I'd printed from a website called yorkshirehistory.com. It gave estimates of the positions of Spurn Point from 600 AD onwards and — after referring back to the OS map — I decided Lod was further south.

I'd just stashed the maps back under my cagoule, when my mobile rang again.

'Hello?'

Silence.

'Hello. Gwen, is that you?'

All I could hear was the sound of the sea, and wind over water.

'Gwen! Is it you?'

'Yes.'

There was a strange sibilance to her speech, but it was definitely Gwen. I should know. 'Where are you?'

'Grant . . . '

She put the phone down again.

For the first time since she left, my hopes are real rather than . . . spurious. I don't want to use the word *imagined*. Two phone calls in two days. She changed her number so I couldn't talk to her, and then changed her address so I couldn't find her, but now *she's* trying to reach *me*. I'd hoped *13 Horror Stories* was a message. Now I know it is.

I first set eyes on Gwen in a pub in Lenton nearly three years ago. She was singing with her band, Land Locked, and she was . . . wonderful. Sheryl Crow meets Alanis Morissette with an English accent, weaving her magic in a lacy, pink floral dress, her long blonde hair offset by a black choker. As soon as they'd finished their set, I bought all three of them a drink, and began a relationship more powerful, fluctuating, and painful than I'd ever imagined possible. There was no equator or mean, only the polar extremes of ecstasy and torment.

For a year or so it was great, despite the lows that inevitably followed the highs. I was still finding my feet as a freelancer, but the work suited me because I'm a nosy, pushy bastard at the best of times. I sold a few articles to the *Express*, *Sun*, and *Guardian*, then a few features to some glossy magazines, and Gwen and I moved in together in a house in West Bridgford. I didn't want to be with her, I wanted to possess her. Her mind, her body, her soul.

Then, last year — her final year of legal apprenticeship — something changed. She changed. Matured, blossomed, I don't know. I tried to drown her with my love, smother her with more and more attention. But the more I tried to make her mine, the more distant she became. It's called the diving reflex in physiology. Immersion in water causes the body to protect itself by switching to energy saving mode. It's an automatic action that takes place in both conscious and unconscious drowning victims, and it was exactly what she did. Whether she knew it or not, she withdrew from me. Although on the surface things seemed unchanged, I knew she was saving energy, marking time until she could draw breath and take her next step.

This is the first time I've spoken aloud about Gwen since she left. The first time I've had the strength to, because of the phone calls.

I walked south for several hundred metres. When I lost sight of the remains of the Battery, I crossed the dune to the dirt track that goes all the way to Spurn

Point. I made good time on the road, which runs very close to the western edge of the spit. I wondered if the marshy flatland on this side was permanent, or if the tide was just out. After about a mile, I took a path to my left, back up the dune and down onto the beach again. A few metres to the south there was a row of about a dozen wooden pillars extending from the beach into the sea. The tallest was only a few centimetres above the sand and I realised it must have been a pier or groyne of some sort, now under water.

I took out both maps as the rain resumed play, really pissing it down. I'd no idea I was going to be caught in East Yorkshire's next cataclysm, but at least I'd had the sense to cover the maps in clear plastic. Between the lighthouse at the end of the spit and my compass, I could work out my position with a fair degree of accuracy. I estimated another couple of hundred metres down the beach before I'd be directly in line with the submarine city.

I trudged on until I came across

something surreal: half a dozen square stones leading into the sea like steps, in a similar fashion to the wooden pillars. They looked like some kind of ineffectual sea defence, although that made no sense. I couldn't tell what size the stones — which appeared to be flint — were, because I could only see their tops protruding from sand and sea. When I reached them, I noticed a completely uncovered flintstone square sitting at the foot of the grassy dune that bordered the beach. Despite a distance of at least twenty metres between the square stone and the first of the buried stones, it was perfectly in line with them, and stood about chest high. I clambered onto it, and stared out to sea.

I'm still here now.

So is Lod, a mile or so to the east.

Inundated, drowned, dead.

★ ★ ★

Saturday the thirtieth of October; later. It was then, on that rock, that the sense of faceless, inevitable doom descended along with the torrent. Twelve hours later, I can't shake it. Perhaps it's the unforgiving devastation of the waters that engulfed Lod, or perhaps I've been unnerved by the county itself. It's a ghostly, ghastly place. There's Lod and the drowned villages and towns, Dane's Dyke, and the Whitby Gothic Weekend all within a few dozen miles of each other. Or maybe I'm just drowning along with the rest of Yorkshire, the few millimetres that disappear each day accelerated by the flood. Maybe that's why I'm still in Easington in this B&B. I know I should've left for Flamborough, but I don't really need to be at Dane's Dyke until tomorrow night.

In case my fears are justified in some way, and someone other than me should listen to this recording, I'd probably better explain about the child and the HPPD.

I didn't really see a child step from behind the road sign on the M62. What I actually saw was the sign collapse or melt into a small, humanoid shape. The black and white square became the head, the metal frame the shoulders, and the sandbags the feet. Then, the road sign walked out across in front of me. I was pretty sure I was hallucinating, but I couldn't be a hundred percent certain in the rain, and I couldn't afford to take the chance. About a quarter of LSD users experience flashbacks, and about a fifth of those develop Hallucinogen Persisting Deception Disorder. What that means is that I'm one of a lucky five percent of hallucinogen users who trips on a weekly basis, sometimes more, even though I haven't had any of the shit for seven years — phone!

That was another call from Gwen, which went like this:

'Hello!'

She said nothing, but I could hear the wash of waves.

'Gwen, talk to me.'

'Grant . . . '

'Are you all right?' Perhaps it was just the sea in the background, but her speech still sounded unnatural, like a hiss.

'Meet me.'

'Now? Where?'

'Tomorrow . . . '

She hung up.

Her voice slipped through my fingers as easily as she'd slipped out of my life. I couldn't hold her then, and I couldn't keep her on the phone now. I tried to drown her, but it was me that drowned.

When she moved out the HPPD got worse. I went from a couple of mild visual distortions a month to half a dozen fullblown bad trips. The irony is I only got into LSD because I thought I was going to be the next Jack Kerouac, a Jim Morrison of journalism. I wasn't, and I'm not. What I am is half mad from years and years of seeing patterns, haloes, and faces where they aren't; stationary objects swaying or sliding across the floor; things growing to giant dimensions or shrinking, like something out of *Alice in Wonderland*.

Truth to tell, I'm fucking sick of it.

★ ★ ★

Sunday the thirty-first of October. It's dusk now and I've been sitting on this flintstone block since noon, waiting for

Gwen to call. I'm soaked through, but I don't care. While I waited, I've been watching the sea, looking for signs of Lod. I've worked out exactly where it is. It's a mile and a half east-south-east of where I am, under the water, submarine and breathless. These stones form a direct line to it, an arrow from Spurn Head to Lod, less than half an hour's walk away. I've been looking for Lod and thinking about Lot. Lot's wife. She turned into a pillar of salt when she disobeyed the angel's command: do not look behind you.

Do not play back the tape.

I played back the tape.

I don't know why, but I listened to the recording I dictated last night. The thing is — the part when the phone rang — it isn't on the tape. I heard myself say *phone*, but I couldn't hear the ring tone. So I checked the log of incoming calls for the last three days. I think I must have deleted them by accident, because I can't find them. I know I didn't imagine those phone calls. I can't have imagined them, because all my hallucinations are visual.

That's how I can always tell what's real and what's imagined if I don't panic; the imagined stuff is never accompanied by a soundtrack.

I *know* I didn't imagine those three calls.

I haven't — I mean I *have* — spoken to Gwen, but she hasn't called to tell me where she is. It's okay, she doesn't need to. It's no coincidence she sent me *that* book. It was a message, one of those games she liked to play. She knew I would come here when I read the book, so this is where she must be. And if she isn't on Spurn Head, then she must be in Lod. I'm confused and I'm not really sure what's going on, but I *know* she's waiting for me in Lod.

The only problem I have is the breathing reflex. An unavoidable instinct of self-preservation that results in a human being fighting to draw breath regardless of how strong the desire to stay submerged is. Something to do with the amount of carbon dioxide in the blood. Half an hour ago I took all the prescription tranquillizers I've got for

147

the HPPD. I haven't used them for ages, but I always carry a box with me — just in case things get out of hand. As soon as I swallowed the last one, I was flooded with a sense of peace. Seven hundred and fifty years ago, there were men in Lod who didn't panic and flee when the waters came. There were men who knew they were at the end of all things, men who were tired of their lives and loves, and just stayed put.

They're probably still there.

A few minutes ago, a sliver of sun slid through the clouds and bathed a strip of ocean in yellow light. It was exactly a mile and a half away in exactly the direction of the stone steps in front of me now.

I'm going to walk down them.

Down to Lod.

Where Gwen is.

Murder in the Minster

Bauer watched the short motorcade halt outside Hofbau Minster. He glanced at his watch — half an hour before midnight — then back through the binoculars. As always, the king travelled with only a small bodyguard of Secret Police. The men were crisp and economical in their movements, and two of them disappeared through the main entrance, a set of monstrous wooden doors. It appeared as if they had been swallowed up in the maw of a skeletal stone beast. Bauer rested the binoculars in his lap and waited.

He stared at the Minster, a compact, misshapen cross in the middle of a snow-covered graveyard, but had to lean closer to the window to see the tops of the spires and tower. They rose so high into the heavens that they seemed unsteady, as if on the brink of toppling over. The thought amused him. He leant back and scanned the road below. Deacon's Lane was empty.

So was Deacon's House, except for Bauer upstairs and the corpse of the custodian downstairs. Sister Antoinette had been a nun in life, and although he despised everything that Roman Catholicism stood for, he hadn't wanted to kill her.

But the stakes were too high to leave anything to chance.

Bauer brushed his knuckles over the ridged, oily flesh on the left side of his face. The burns were over ten years old, courtesy of Brigadier Rassendyll, the Englishman who was head of the Secret Police. Bauer had shot him in the throat in return, but the bastard had survived. The luck of the devil. He'd been hunting Bauer and his Resistance ever since, each seeking to exterminate the other. But Rassendyll wasn't here tonight. Tonight Bauer would end their long, grim duel all on his own.

He lifted the binoculars as one of the bodyguards returned to the motorcade. Two by two, the rest took up their positions, covering all three entrances to the Minster. A man in a grey cape, with dark red hair and a black eye patch, debussed from the middle car. Rudolf Elphberg, or King Rudolf the Sixth of Ruritania as he was known to the world. Bauer watched him stride into the great, gaping mouth alone. A few seconds later, the other bodyguard joined his colleagues outside the Minster, closing the huge door behind him.

Bauer moved quickly. He dropped the binoculars and headed for the stairs, touching the butt of his pistol for luck. Down past the corpse, and down again to the wine cellar. He had already raised the flagstone in the middle of the floor, and a torch and crowbar lay on either side of the square of darkness under the raw, sodium light. He knelt, took hold of the torch, and lowered himself into the narrow excavation. The uneven walls were slick with moisture and the tunnel was so low he had to crouch down. Later, he would have to crawl for about twenty feet.

He knew this because he'd already made the journey once, last week.

Bauer groped his way along through the belly of the earth: under Deacon's Lane, under the graveyard, under the chapter house, and then under the north wall of the Minster. He was shivering and caked with grime when he arrived at the end of the passage. Rusty iron rungs were riveted to the foundation blocks, and he used them to climb up into a priest's hole. It was so small that there was only half a flagstone of floor space. He squeezed into it, switched off the torch, and was immediately enveloped in a complete and impenetrable darkness. He shuddered, feeling the weight of the tons of stone pressing in on him. The icy hand of fear closed around his heart and he forced a cough to get his lungs working again.

Bauer squatted and very carefully set the torch down between his feet. He placed both of his hands flat on the stone in front of him and felt for the small indentation. He found it a minute later, and pushed hard with two stiff, dirty fingers. The door rasped as it opened, revealing shadows dancing and twisting on the limestone wall. He could hear a voice echoing from the right — the bishop. He stood, drew his pistol, and screwed the silencer onto the end of the barrel. Then he stepped out into the niche, leaving the concealed door open behind him. Everyone knew about the priest's hole and the three hundred year old emergency exit. They also knew that the tunnel had been impassable since part of it collapsed in 1877.

They were wrong.

Bauer looked out from the niche, at the tomb of Marshal Strackenz — Ruritania's greatest soldier — sitting stolid under a decorative canopy. The sanctuary was illuminated by a faint light filtering through the quatrefoils, and the flickering of candles beyond the choir screen. He couldn't help gazing up the thin, needle-like columns opposite, to their teetering capitals, and the great ribbed arches of the ceiling. He felt his balance start to go, and averted his eyes as he steadied himself. He poked his head out from the niche. To his left, the apse was small, dark, and empty. To his right, the choir screen effectively blocked his view of the nave. More importantly, it blocked the views of the king and the bishop on the other side. Bauer slipped out into the sanctuary, and stole towards the nave, using the aisle formed by the clustered columns.

It had taken him two years to find out where Elphberg attended Midnight Mass. Two years and three of Rassendyll's men tortured to death. The first had been brave, incredibly so. He'd screamed like a pig, but he'd told them nothing. His death was slow and painful. The Resistance had bungled the second interrogation. It was Bauer's fault for leaving it to one of his lieutenants. The man was determined to extract the information, but his brutality proved counter-productive when he killed the prisoner by accident. Bauer had taken charge of the third himself. The policeman parted with the location after five hours: a private ceremony conducted by the Bishop of Hofbau in the country's smallest cathedral. Then a fast drive to Zenda, where the king issued his Christmas message to the nation at one o'clock precisely.

Not tonight.

As Bauer passed the north transept, he flexed his fist around the butt of his pistol and smiled. The weapon was a product of their Czech neighbours, the most reliable handgun in the world. He had already killed five men and one woman with it, and he knew it wouldn't fail him. He glided past the choir screen and into the nave. The hundreds of candles cast more shadow than light, and the stained glass windows only increased the effect. Bauer looked up at the clerestory. The richly moulded ribs supporting the ogive-arched vault looked like the bones of a leviathan seen from the inside. He couldn't help feeling small and insignificant — just like the priests intended — until he caught sight of Elphberg, kneeling before the bishop at the high altar.

Tonight Bauer was neither small nor insignificant: he was the instrument of the destruction of the Royal House of Elphberg.

He eased behind a column, keeping to the shadows. He held his pistol loosely in both hands — ready for the kill — and examined Elphberg, now only a dozen feet away. Unlike most of Europe's parasites, Rudolf dressed simply. He wore the scarlet tunic, white breeches, and black cavalry boots of the King's Royal Cuirassiers — of which he was Colonel-in-Chief — with only two decorations. Around his throat, the Order of the Red Rose of Ruritania, worn by all the aristocracy, and on his chest, a lone medal; a memento of his military service in Britain, where the Elphbergs had chosen exile over the new People's Republic.

Like most of his ancestors, Rudolf had a shock of dark red hair and a prominent, elongated nose. But it was the eye patch that now dominated his features. Bauer recalled the ambush, three years ago, as if it was yesterday. He and five of the Resistance had launched a rocket-propelled grenade at the royal limousine. Prince Rupert, the nine year old Duke of Strelsau, had been killed instantly, along with everyone else — all except Rudolf. Like Rassendyll, he had the luck of the devil. But the attack hadn't been wasted; it had deprived him of his only heir and his right eye.

In the land of the blind the one-eyed man is king.

Not for much longer. Once the

Elphbergs were gone, the darkness would lift, and the people would embrace socialist democracy again. Bauer eased back the hammer of his pistol, and rested his right forefinger on the trigger. Elphberg stood and the bishop blessed him a final time. He offered his hand to the bishop and they shook. A modern king indeed, but still a throwback to the oppression of the absolute monarch. He turned to leave the Minster.

Bauer stepped from the aisle and raised his pistol. Elphberg stopped dead. The bishop — startled — clasped his hands tight under his violet maniple. Bauer focused on the bridge of Elphberg's nose through the front sight of his pistol.

Something was wrong.

The eye patch was on the right hand side. Bauer's right, Rudolf's left — but that wasn't right. Bauer lowered his pistol slightly and squinted in the half-light. The nose was fake. So was the red hair.

Rassendyll.

'I tortured three of your men for this. How did you do it?'

Rassendyll spoke softly. 'Only three

men knew about tonight. His Majesty, me — '

'And the bishop.' Bauer glanced up at him. But it wasn't the Bishop of Hofbau, it was someone else, and that someone had produced a pistol from under his maniple.

' . . . And Reverend Father Sapt, Chaplain-Major of the Royal Defence Force.'

'Drop it, Bauer,' said Sapt, 'it's over.'

'I thought priests were forbidden to kill.'

'In your case, I'm prepared to risk eternal damnation.'

Bauer saw a flash of movement from Rassendyll and when he turned back, the policeman was pointing a small pistol at him. 'The eye patch. I should've realised.'

'A necessary risk. My left eye isn't good enough for a clear shot in this light.'

'Did you know I'd use the tunnel?' Bauer asked.

'What tunnel?'

Bauer was tempted to kill Rassendyll anyway, regardless of the consequences. It would be suicide. Satisfying, certainly, but ultimately pointless. On the other hand, he'd already escaped from the Secret Police once before, and he knew he could do it again. He lowered his weapon, dropped it, and raised his palms.

Sapt covered his pistol, and began reciting, 'Our Father, who art in heaven, hallowed be Thy name. Thy kingdom come. Thy will be done, on earth as it is in heaven . . . '

Rassendyll said, 'God save the king.'

' . . . Give us this day our daily bread, and forgive us our trespasses . . . '

Bauer had his second revelation of the night an instant before the bullet penetrated his skull. He fell, his head hit the hard stone, and he knew no more.

Sapt made the sign of the cross over him. 'As we forgive those who trespass against us. And lead us not into temptation, but deliver us from evil . . . '

Rassendyll knelt down and placed two fingers on Bauer's throat. He felt the pulse and the life slowly ebb away.

' . . . For Thine is the kingdom, and the power, and the glory, forever and ever. Amen.' Sapt stepped down from the dais

are all out of water and I'm ashamed to say I took more than my fair share.

I lost consciousness several more times while we made our escape, and it has been my only respite from the pain. The sniper fire has increased since we stopped and I expect a sortie any minute. I'm too weak to hold a rifle, but I have my side-arm slung across my chest like some Mexican bandit. I realise now I was a fool to have volunteered for action. I could have stayed with my regiment in relative safety, but I chose not to. It was a reckless decision, and I can hardly complain now that the danger I sought out has found me. But I will not wallow in self-pity. I am determined to give a good account of myself if I am conscious when the final assault comes, be it here or some other place.

I hope my nerve will not fail me.

We will be moving again shortly, making for Haut-i-Madat. From there we will try to reach the Argandab River in darkness, but I doubt I'll last that long. The terrain is more rugged and inhospitable than I imagined. I thought our superior technology would give us an advantage over the enemy, but I was wrong. There appears to be no flat land in this country. It is all either steep mountains, or steep valleys. I've always prided myself on my fitness, but rugby training was no preparation for the altitude and the heat and the dust. Not that it would have made any difference today after the wound. Even if I managed to survive this battle, my rugger days would be over.

Another shot, closer this time. It's so strange, but aside from water, I absolutely crave a cigar. One of the Dutch imports my tobacconist sends. I don't suppose I'll ever have another one of them now. Nor will I ever visit his shop in Long Lane again. Or see London again. I feel that my medical training should have prepared me for death, but it hasn't. I've seen hundreds of people die of many different causes, but it doesn't make my own death any more palatable. I just can't imagine not being alive anymore. Not being. I don't want to imagine it. I want to live a long life.

I can see Murray coming back. We'll be moving shortly, and I'll be slung back over the horse. I'm going to give this letter to him now. If anyone here makes it home, he will. Don't ever doubt the strength of my feelings for you. Remember me well.

Your loving brother,
John H. Watson
Captain-Surgeon, Army Medical Service
27th July 1880